THE FIRST 38

THE FIRST

A shotgun array of short stories

Bill McCluskey

THE FIRST 38
A SHOTGUN ARRAY OF SHORT STORIES

iUniverse books may be ordered through booksellers or by contacting:

iUniverse
1663 Liberty Drive
Bloomington, IN 47403
www.iuniverse.com
1-800-Authors (1-800-288-4677)

ISBN: 978-1-4917-6175-5 (sc)
ISBN: 978-1-4917-6176-2 (e)

Print information available on the last page.

iUniverse rev. date: 04/15/2015

ACKNOWLEDEMENTS

A very special thanks to my lovely wife, Annah, my sister, Rosalie, and our two very helpful cats.

CONTENTS

COIFFURE LOVE

Edgar's handcrafted Italian leather loafers fidgeted while he leaned over the finger marked glass display case. The third scissors from the left, the mirror finished, polished stainless steel short ones, a thirty-five dollar white price tag dangled, then disappeared, a done deal.

Edgar, a Boston born thirty-one year old, a conservative accountant with a national firm, lives moderately well on the second level of a Brownstone hardwood floor flat. Life is good but lonely and he has too few friends. Edgar frets and worries about his heavily starched, gold cuff linked, pin striped, Rolex watched self imposed corral. Socially shy, yet attractive, Edgar longs to live the many mysteries of love with his unfound soul mate goddess.

The German ground precision scissors would clip his few errant, scrawling, black nasal hairs and hopefully present Edgar as more appealing, a classier chunk of dangling social bait.

A long legged, swan necked contemporary dancer, Vanessa, twenty-eight, movement intense with a dose of that "crazier than a shit house rat" occasional behavior that is secretly injected into all passionate dancers. A natural blonde with one of those lanky, sculpted bodies straight off the photo cover of one of those skin cream, hair care advertisements.

Vanessa barely squeaked by on the last of her scholarship money, waitress by day, dance by night, thank God Uncle Earl was traveling. The lower floor of the leather furnished Brownstone was a gracious retreat from her over disciplined dance world.

Too busy and dance fatigued, she slumped completely into the comforting surround of the Conroy leather chair. Here sat Vanessa, vibrant, energetic and passionate in a new city, yet lonely for a full time love man, tired and nearly broke.

The lightly sandblasted Boston Backbay Brownstone was an architectural delight: heavy speckled Vermont granite worn entry stairs, deeply projecting stone window sills, relieved carved brass trimmed entry doors with identical floor plans, Vanessa at ground level and Edgar above.

They had cordially offered a bread and butter "Hello" as they occasionally passed at the entry, Edgar always holding his breath as he side surveyed the depth of Vanessa's beauty. She smiled as Edgar swiftly moved to display his best southern coachman like door opening manners. A sparkling, white toothed thank you and a wink. Edgar's love bell rang with leaping love images, conjured up during the everything is possible early love beginnings.

Had his recent nasal hair trimming finally exposed the romantic Edgar; smiling, he slept and dreamt of the lovely Vanessa, also alone in her poster bed, exactly and sadly, one floor below.

As Edgar soundly slept, moonlight sculpted to his ivory pillow as it began, at first like an expected flash of movement from the corner of his nostril. Then again, this time several coarse black hairs grew slowly from each of Edgar's openings, slowly but surely moving cautiously over his lip and chin like a raven-black out-of-control Jack in the Beanstalk.

The nocturnal appearing hairs retreated after each night's excursions, first limited to the edge of Edgar's bed, but now inclusive of the entire flat.

As Edgar's aggressive night shift hair outings emboldened, Vanessa was also experiencing a moonlit hair renaissance during her dancing, moon ivory slumber. At first a spring curled locket of glistening blonde hair, then another, springing a well watered hair forest between her long legged ivory smooth, rose petaled thighs. Like finely twisted golden coils of sunsets, her exploratory hair slipped from beneath her silk camisole to the floor. Lightly coiling around objects, the long golden strands, like thousands of golden serpent tongues, weave-darting around the piano legs, glass domed light and glowing tropical fish tank.

Both Edgar and Vanessa's nightly hair curiosity expeditions led each respective hair alliance to the edge of their known frontier, the Brownstone exterior window sills, boundary edge of the known hair world.

The humid, full mooned Boston night, floor fans humming, ice packs thawing and the hair colonies, one lustered raven black, the other ringlets of platinum coiled moon gold.

The moonlit machine wire cut limestone exterior facade, provided a perfect stage between Vanessa's and Edgar's windows.

The advance scout hairs were first onto and beyond the open window sills. Curling and bending like cautious hairs should, the vigilant scout hairs suddenly sensing opposite colored hairs approaching.

Hopeful cordialities were exchanged, as hair scouts often do, and opposite colored hairs began to socialize, straight lined at first but then in curled, coiled, teased and rolled couplings like

Byzantine columns, an alternating moonlit gold braided with raven black.

The hair colonies celebrated their fortunate moon gathering by forming intricate doily laced hair stranded designs, involving thousands of opposites hairs, concluding with a decorative braided tower complete with blonde filigree and looped curled black hair trim.

Totally unified, both colonies gracefully s-curved to Vanessa's palomino covered stone window sill, paused, then cascaded over the beveled wood window molding, down the curved base to a straight smooth hardwood floor expressway directly to her bedroom.

Lost in the moonlit stains of slow motion dreams, Vanessa's alabaster smooth limbs were veiled with a thin gauze of woven hair, delicate as a spider's glistening web.

Effectively Vanessa's body was slowly cocooned in a sturdy net of woven hairs then smoothly moved to the window sill in a formal ritual hair colony processional, complete with rolled flanking curls, braided rings and supporting spit curls.

Engineering Corps hairs had pre-rigged the hair pulley and Vanessa was steadily elevated to Edgar's bedroom window sill. Heavy lifting curls glided Vanessa to Edgar's bedside, lifting her, then carefully placing her in Edgar's deep sleep embrace as softly as a butterfly.

Their magical task completed, the satisfied hair colonies slowly retreated, promising to meet again, informally and close up, in the very near future.

CLUCKING TIMMY

Timothy J. Calder, Jr., named after his grandfather, Timothy, Sr., credited with the invention of the ceramic oscilloscope, was not exactly tracking in grandpa's footsteps.

Both parents pridefully beamed at Timmy, their only son, at the center of his seventh year garden birthday party. Surrounded in the lush private landscape of their upper class Darian, Connecticut, estate, Timmy was smothered with parental admonitions, sugar dripping with an endless array of adolescent opportunities: tutors from Hartford, tedious and often nerve shattering violin lessons from Olga, private soccer instructions from that dirty nailed Brazilian, Felipe, and those endless mathematical quizzes from the chuckling Dr. Kane.

Yeh, past, present and future, Timmy had his detailed life road map carefully scripted, measured in quarter ounce servings from birth to death by his overly concerned parents, Alfred and Charlotte, the ever dial tuning navigators of the Timmy life boat. Overly protected and socially filtered, Timmy had access to only invited playmates; and as Alfred and Charlotte looked over the sugar-sticky, sun drenched party, they cooed child rearing congratulations under the willow capped white gazebo.

Timmy quietly stood several steps from his imported friends, locked onto the manicured grass turf, he gazed unflinchingly at the ice cream dripping frenzy of his age, all charged with the sugar of the raspberry layer cake.

His clear blue eyes contrasted with his fiery red hair, freshly razor cut by Charles of Darian and perfectly comb molded to his globe shaped head. The crisp blue gem sparkle of his silver birth ring glinted as he methodically tapped his well scrubbed fingers. Slightly swaying, Timmy claw hooked his pudgy thumbs through the belt loops of the buff grey Lederhauser shorts, the ones with the blue and green embroidery on the suspenders that Grandma brought him from Switzerland.

He knew he was different from the rest, yet kept it to himself, silently observing the behavior of others.

A week or so after the party, Charlotte and Alfred drove upstate to visit an extensive dairy and chicken farm owned by Alfred's cousin, Vernon. This annual weekend provided Timmy with one of his planned nature dousings and exposed him to farm boy realities from the other corner of his all too calibrated world.

Timmy always took to Vernon, shadowing his every farm task from sun up to dinner. Bib-overall clad Vernon was quiet, yet polite, and always paused to answer Timmy's unending questions: "No, only the girl cows give milk; they usually lay their eggs early morning, and pigs wallow in it because they stay cooler and attract fewer flies."

After their first day, it became clear that Timmy had a strong fascination with the ever hungry pecking chickens, and Vernon let Timmy scatter feed twice a day. Timmy loved his new farm responsibility, feeder of the chickens, and carefully scattered feed in a clucking world of bobbing yellow beaks, tomato red crowns, rust colored feathers and those skinny, prehistoric like taloned feet, the ones with the very sharp tips, so necessary for dirt scratching.

By the third day Timmy entered the largest chicken coop and remained until dinner time, not even the noon time deep dish apple pie aroma from the covered kitchen porch could sway his dedication to the strutting cacklers.

Timmy sat, legs spread on the dirt packed floor of the ventilated coop, down at the level of the chickens where feeding became more intimate, eye to eye with the plumed tail roosters.

Timmy noticed the rare stillness of the largest rooster, rather than greedily plucking feed from the apron bib, he locked eyes with Timmy and there seemed to be an instant, unexplainable connection between the two, a kind of linkage only possible between a child and chicken, one of deep respect for the other.

Late afternoon, as Vernon approached the coop, he noticed all the clucking had subsided, except for the largest rooster that now sat beside Timmy in the corner clucking strange sounds directly into his left ear. Timmy's eyes widened as the now excited rooster endlessly clucked. Everything instantly stopped as Vernon's weathered hand reached for the varmit proof door latch, then all chickens resumed pecking and only the strange gazing of the large rooster seemed out of place.

As they walked to the white clapboard farmhouse, Vernon noticed a trickling blood droplet on Timmy's right wrist, "It's ok, I'm a big boy; that large rooster pecked me when you came in."

Back home everything appeared in balance, the wealthy humdrum of a cradled existence, yet there were changes. At first, hardly noticeable, Timmy began to spend more time alone in his room, reading everything he could find regarding the life of chickens. "Curious, must just be a passing fancy from Vernon's farm; it will pass," mused the parents.

Slowly, some of Timmy's life habits began to change: he drew numerous profiles of chickens in his sketchbook and taped them on his bedroom walls, sometimes laughing and mumbling clucking sounds at his drawings.

Outwardly, Timmy began to mock the staccato movements of chickens, quickly jerking his head from side to side, especially while in the garden, removing his shoes and repeatedly digging into the deep piled carpet with his toes while making that clucking sound from the back of his throat.

At mealtime Timmy only seemed to prefer corn, anything with grain or seeds in it and lots of leafy lettuce. Alfred and Charlotte were mortified as Timmy surprisingly dropped his dinner fork and proceeded to peck vegetables from the edge of his gold leafed, bone china plate.

In new found despair, his parents slowly opened his heavy oaken bedroom door, there, clutching the scrolled footboard of his antique bed was Timmy, nude and making that deep throated clucking sound. With a glossed over look he rose, flapped his arms and took flight to the inlaid parquet floor. Astonished, Alfred and Charlotte gingerly placed Timmy in bed, provided hugs, warm milk, left the Teddy Bear nightlight on and called the family doctor from the privacy of the den.

Dr. Chandler, all the way from Hartford, pulled into the cobble stoned turnaround nearly two hours later and discussed symptoms with the parents before visiting Timmy.

"He's been acting so strangely since our visit to Vernon's farm, as if something has come over him: pecks his food at the table, makes loud clucking sounds at daybreak, recently drinks only from the fish pond, uses the lawn as his toilet and we just can't keep popcorn in the house."

As the three entered Timmy's room they knew something was amiss. The bed sheets had telltale tattered edges and the open window framed a slashed screen as if it had been pecked. Fuzz like small feathers caught the light evening breeze and slowly carouseled to the floor near Timmy's quickly discarded favorite cowboy pajamas, a ring of feathers still stuck to the elastic waistband. The exterior security lights highlighted fresh tracks trailing across the glistening grass, not shoe prints, but the triangular tracks of a large bird.

Heartbroken, Alfred and Charlotte combed the immediate countryside, hired professionals and worked closely with law enforcement, all to no avail. Little Timmy, their life's pride, had mysteriously vanished without a trace, without a whimper. After months of fruitless investigations, Timmy Calder, Jr., was officially listed as a missing child.

Charlotte and Alfred decided to visit Vernon's farm late that summer for a change of heart and scenery, even though they knew the farm was once very special for their only Timmy. Following the annual tour, Charlotte visited the chicken coop Timmy loved so well.

Alone at the feeding bench she initially disregarded the mindless direction and clucking of the chickens, at least until things grew silent. Then, very calmly and slowly the chickens gravitated to the far corner of the large, metal roofed coop, that is, all but the two largest roosters. The two green iridescent plumed roosters slowly strutted side by side toward Charlotte, stopping within an arm's length without a flinch.

Charlotte admired the rooster on the left, he was here during Timmy's last visit, the one Vernon laughingly described as giving Timmy an ear full.

Her breath shortened and she bit her glossed lower lip while eyeing the other rooster. It seemed to be coddling her ankle and affectionately brushing tail feathers against her lower calf. Silently the rooster peered into Charlotte's face through those lucid blue eyes, the only blue eyes in the entire coop, with that look of compassion that only few chickens have. And there banded on the left leg, the blue gem sparkle of Timmy's silver birth ring.

Charlotte flooded with tears, didn't tell a soul and returned to the coop daily carefully observing every nuance of the blue eyed rooster.

The Bentley was packed with the matching leather luggage and Charlotte made her very last trip to the chicken coop. She sat on the bench as all the clucking and fine ginger color dust settled. Slowly, from the corner, the sole blue eyed rooster approached and fluttered to the bench. Lightly cooing, the rooster laid his head in the curve of Charlotte's palm and stared the look of blue eyed understanding. Charlotte, lightly stroked the ornate tail feathers as only a mother can, slowly rose and rode home in absolute silence.

The blue eyed rooster marveled at the gift left for him on the worn oak bench, a neatly piled pyramid of dried yellow corn and two small candy bars. Oh yea, candy bars with nuts.

GROUND ZERO

During my bubble gum years, my sister and I were furloughed to my conservative, Pennsylvania Dutch grandparents' in New Philadelphia, Ohio, the cradle of Presbyterian and Mennonite values. These annual one week episodes provided my parents a brief romantic getaway and gave us parental freedom and adventure.

My grandfather owned an out of city coal and building supply yard and I lived to spend the day among the heavy platform truck scale, coal laden rail cars and rusting steel conveyors. The place spoke to sweat, dust, muscle and back breaking work, a good fit for my hard working grandfather, covered in grim and sweat, sometimes solely moving a loaded coal car with a well worn timber spar.

We lunched in the oppressive heat of the shed office on great home prepared food and steel ladled, natural cool spring water.

One sizzling August afternoon he abruptly declared that overdue bill collection was at hand and we set out to the downtown area to retrieve his hard earned cash. It seemed curious to me that his services would be needed in this seedy, hard edged area.

Gold toothed, slicked, pretty boy pimps with wildly colored feather cocked hats buttressed the grime stained, going out of business street front merchants, each propped at the door with their half pint of browned bag liquor.

He heeled the truck curbside, parking almost directly in front of a open-doors bar, noisy with chatter, clicking glasses, laughter, blues music, smoke and alcohol - all endlessly wafting to the street. "This is a serious area," he said, "remain in the truck, keep the windows up and the doors locked, I'll return in a few minutes." According to the cracked dash clock, promised minutes slowly dragged to an hour.

The truck cab interior became my caged playground, a vinyl seated, coal dust veiled mechanical cavern fully outfitted with shifters, knobs, dials and all the Tonka dump truck stuff. I slid behind the wheel and practiced my driving moves, adding my own amplified acoustics. Mid shift I noticed an agonizing pressure in my bowels, the rumbling kind alerting you that something is on its way - and soon.

Warned to remain in the locked truck I now desperately needed a bathroom. I could stand it no longer and something deep down was telling me that immediate action was required.

After snapping the chrome buttoned dash box latch, I removed my grandfather's neatly folded red work handkerchief, the kind cowboys sometimes tie around their necks for sweat and dust. I smoothed the unfolded linen target on the rider's side floor mat,ground zero, the center of the red field.

In a lurch of fear and embarrassment I ankled my jeans and shorts, squatting in the cramped seat well, praying no one would pass by and I relieved myself, fortunately dead on target.

As I rose, the perilous impossibility: my grandfather and his newly found partner quite untimely emerged from the bar within several feet of the truck. I froze, then quickly folded my floor sculpture into a mounded square and delicately placed it atop the road maps, transforming the dash box to its new found chemical toilet status.

Righting his checkered, coal dusted wool hat, he stepped into the late afternoon sunlight, vacuum locked to a giggling, twentyish, dusty street wise mulatta, the kind with legally borderline, dollar dredging, hunting instincts.

This shapely young Negras, too tipsy to walk, hugged against my grandfather in a python like s-curve. She hip gyrated her pelvis in a fashion that was a cross between the ritual Blackhawk Indian Eagle Dance and lap dancing at a Dallas titty bar.

There they swayed alright, America's most unlikely couple.

A light pat on the rump, a final whispered giggle and the sultry pleasure princess disappeared back into her thumping, neon den.

Peeling a roll of breathmints while climbing into the cab, he mumbled that these collections take time and he might need to return in a few days. Windows quickly down, engine humming, we were on our way.

The knobby, sun cracked tires of the ten ton Dodge whined into the heat softened asphalt as we turned homeward over a series of ribboned hills.

Wide open window and vents provided a steady stream of refreshing sweet corn Ohio air each time we throttled down hill.

Up hill was an entirely different environment. As the truck groaned during the incline challenges, a gauze like blue clutch smoke rose from the cab floor as he continually down shifted the never satisfied gears. More importantly, the flow of fresh air subsided and we were repeatedly overtaken by the then harsh stable odor thinly camouflaged in the truck dash box.

I stared straight ahead as our nostrils were assaulted with every hill. Not a word was spoken on our way home yet his glance told me he knew the stink monster was somewhere on board.

Heavily panting, the truck was finally bedded behind the white washed tool shed. As we rolled to a lurching stop I instantly shattered the land speed record for truck exiting. I quick stepped through the garden toward the house and decided to chance a quick rear glance as I reached the staked tomatoes.

There it was alright, one of those indelible life snap shots, the kind that reside forever in your number one brain memory cells. Standing beside the open rider's door, my grandfather stood frozen, locked into studying the newly found contents of his red handkerchief spread upwards on his palms like a church hymnal.

I scrubbed and languished in the water of the upstairs oversized, claw footed bathtub until my skin wrinkled. Anything to prolong any dreaded dinner confrontation. Finally, I slinked to the dining room, guided only by floor and ceiling vision, avoiding my grandfather's now curious gaze.

Noting an uncommon dinner time silence, my grandmother asked, "Did you have a good day at the yard?"

My grandfather responded mincingly between bites of fresh green beans, "Well.... we had a fair day.... except Billy got a little sick on the way home."

FILIPINO CULTURE

Filipino skin glistens differently in the glittering, gold dust, sunset; there is a certain light sienna tint that reflects beads of perspiration on sun bleached hair. In fact, the skin tone glows with a sense of pride, Filipino pride, blood line true and forever irreversible.

I silently eyed my precious wife and daughters as they basked in the slowly dissolving sunset, inhaling the last of the sun's salt sprayed heat, that special time when things magically turn pinkish purple, just before fire time.

The never changing stone lined fire ring provided heat for our family cooking and served as our outside gathering spot, four sets of giggling brown eyes in the fire light, Filipina dough wrapped spice meat on the fire flat pan, evening stars growing with every glance and squeals of laughter shuffled with serious speak - life is good.

Three generations now on the island, same green painted beach cottage house, same palm and koa trees, same Filipino pride, first grandpa, then dad and now me.

Granpa Arturo, thin mustached in the collared shirt, that's him in the faded photograph hanging by the wooden crucifix. Labor immigrant from Manila with the white man's promises of independent wealth and respect; grandpa arrived with his wife and pride during the late 1920s to a life of cane field stoop work. He and his wife's backs achingly bent, but their pride stood stubbornly tall. Barely subsiding, life consisted of a single room labor shack with corrugated tin roof, hand carried water, lantern light, demeaning white skinned labor bosses and drowning debt at the plantation owner's goods store.

Burning thin cane cuts left hands and feet stinging, bodies racked and disfigured from stoop cutting and loading, mules pulling tracked refinery cane cars, steam engines and the constant haze of burning fields mingled with sweat, tears and the feelings of trapped hopelessness. Bosses preached a brighter future that never came and grandpa died early of over work and a heavy heart, but died gripping his Filipino pride.

My father was doggedly determined to improve family conditions and live only in granpa's house until he landed a better job. Stoop labor and cane fields were slowly giving way to hotel and tourist destination developments. My father rambled and dreamed of managing a hotel or being head barman at the newest resort, an evening of tips would be more than granpa made in an entire month.

My father and mother sat dejected in our tiny kitchen, dressed in their finest and only Filipino style white linen and lace. The new hotel interview man had ushered them through the rear service delivery entry, hotel laborers could not be seen or enter the main stone floored lobby. Once inside, they were promptly escorted to the kitchen and maid service quarters and told all jobs were based on performance. "Well, maybe someday you will manage this hotel or be the evening barman," snickered the white boss man, "but until then you will wash dishes, you know, a hotel pearl diver and you will clean guest toilets, change linens and be fired if late or caught stealing hotel soap or food."

My parents slaved at the resort hotel while their thick black Filipino hair thinned and slowly grayed. After decades of scraping garbage and scouring toilets we still lived in granpa's cottage, nourished only by family and the ever present Filipino pride.

As our third generation island Filipino, I was resolved to finding a better life for myself and family. I registered for computer training and began classes, a ray of hope, white collar job and respect from my current burger flipping colleagues at the oil saturated, fast food chain.

After my fourth class, we learned that my older daughter had developed a seriously spreading staff infection in her left ankle. Stern looking doctors suggested intricate and prohibitively expensive surgery and us with only $17.00 carefully folded in a glass jar and without insurance.

Looking tenderly at my daughter, I felt it rising, expanding my rib cage, the heritage of my Filipino pride.

With the highest intentions and the lowest hard hitting realities, I saw three proud generations, leaving granpa a hard scrabble stoop worker, dad a dishwasher pearl diver and me, the real burger king. Our world was overdue for major changes.

Backing my neighbors borrowed, rusty fendered, older Toyota pick up into the stall near the parking lot entry, I focused on the aluminum framed entry doors of the Island State Bank. I deeply exhaled, mentally documenting the last of my nervous before moments, leaving the key in the ignition and slid from the seat.

Feinting a casual walk, I squeezed the ski mask in my left hand into a compact, palm sized, sweat dampened ball and carefully adjusted the non slip pistol grip of the Smith-Wesson 357 caliber revolver in my waist band, covered by my favorite palm pattern Aloha shirt and with renewed and a much fairer Filipino pride, headed for the teller line.

JUNGLE BIRD

My lightly oil sheened wings arched wider, symmetrically forming a blue black gentle s-curve of tier lapped feathers, opening slowly and mysteriously as a Ming Dynasty tea ceremony fan.

My wing muscles relaxed as the humid, warm thermal air mass lifted me upward, higher above the steaming tropical South American rain forest. Below, like a million upright umbrellas, damp, richly green domes of the forest canopy of Banyan, Monkeypod, Mahogany and hardwoods, provided an aviary dream world for my wanderlust style as a wandering Toucan.

Life is good, predators few, fruit, water and leafy shelter are bountiful, but as a loner I must admit some companionship would be welcomed. Not just any old fly by night bird and not too jabbery or having a sexual thing about female Toucans with overly developed bright yellow beaks, but, one of those rare kind of gentle sorts with an understanding heart.

After three mid day gliding hours, rest and nourishment were calling and I French curve descended above a grove of sweet budding mangos. An unexpected small clearing, a light tan punctuation dot in an endless light green leafy sea, complete with a small rusting corrugated tin roof, several wood crates, one chair and a tattered canopy molded and rotted from the ever decaying damp padded forest floor.

I gingerly perched on the edge of a juice stained fruit crate, quickly scoped the shack, then, like magic I spotted them - a shoe box sized treasure of shelled cashew nuts - the Goddess of the nuts was kind today. My favorite treat and only three short hops away; my beak salivated as I crisply snapped down three absolutely delicious beauties and perched for my feast.

Eduardo, a mid aged outcast tribal Indian, moved slowly toward me, smoothly, almost as gliding. His open palms outstretched as he soothingly hummed an ancient tribal song. With an ever broadening smile and deep wet brown eyes, he graciously offered more cashews, water and cut fruits. I trusted him immediately, perched myself on the back of his sole worn bamboo chair and we traded life stories, laughs, screeches, tears and wonderful amazement. Eduardo was a kind spirit and tenderly understood the way of Toucans.

Who would ever guess that we would fall in love, marry and have our proud offspring; and to think it all started with a little nut. Our fondness for each other ripened to love as did the moist, colorful yellow and red orange fruits of the thickest jungle. He was simple, honest and affectionately showed me great kindness. In the hot jungle days and moon filled nights, we fell deeply into the joys of love.

Steamy jungle night sounds and a full magical moon just above the leaves of those mangos, I slowly combed his chest hairs with my beak as he delicately stroked my tail feathers, occasionally nubbing my appreciating beak. Life is good.

Our at first awkward love making had now drummed to the truly breathtaking level, and one exceptionally passionate jungle night we began our son.

During the later months of pregnancy, my once muscle toned body gave way to a more bulbous Toucan that could barely fly. I was also crankier, craving wild honey dipped yaha berries. Eduardo was totally and lovingly supportive.

Biologically and technically strange, yes, but not impossible. That sonogram did have some very interesting profiles. National Geographic photographers arrived with a gynecologist and we proudly presented our cooing new son. It most certainly surprised the visiting doctor; he said it was a first, a man and a Toucan bearing a child. Not just any child but a unique, happy, bubbling baby boy.

He definitely has my beak but Eduardo's eyes, my wings with his ears and, of course, my long winged tail. He was given the best nest fed organic worms, fresh fruit, seeds and the tenderest of bugs all delivered with loving care.

We finally located a native jungle school within flying distance. So difficult to find a school that teaches both skipping and flying, pecking with reading and a sports program suitable for our modified Toucan.

He enjoys school immensely, plays with native Indians and loves basketball, although once accused of deflating the winning opponent's ball with a lightning fast beak tip slash. Additionally, he once feverishly pecked the cafeteria vending machine glass lense to access a packet of Brazilian nuts. He's a great little guy.

I'm off to find a stroller with a seat hole for tail feathers and the fly is long. As I lock in my wings, the caressing scented thermal lifts me higher and I set in for a long, relaxing dead still glide, needle cutting through the silent, sun molecule particled, thick jungle air floating above my happy fulfilled Toucan life.

MODERN ART

My first bau-relief carving never made it to the museum of modern art but was never the less famous and unforgotten by my family.

At four years old, my father presented me with one of my first male Rites of Passage, a clasped, lapiz blue, big guy's pen knife.

It was given with my father's anticipated, "Don't cut yourself, open it this way," instructions and a distinctive rolling of my mother's eyes that translated, "He's too young for this."

The knife and I became the closest of friends, bridging my boasting right to all male buddies if I would just keep it clean and sharp and under my pillow each night, next to the trusty Roy Roger's cap pistol.

The Chippendale desk was a favorite, a family pass on collector's piece from Grandma's. The knee space provided a secret hiding place with the chair pulled in giving me occasional peeps at my sister's and mother's legs as they passed.

The smooth, stained furniture face with its hard lacquered finish provided a perfect palette for my ambitious pen knife carvings. For hours I diligently toiled delighted with the ice skate like movement of the hungry blade. These artistic strokes of genius were often accented with heavy gouges similar to French cave paintings, an interpretive feast for any child psychiatrist.

After several silent but industrious days of sculpting I considered the master piece complete.

Discovery came surely and quickly in the midst of ritual Pennsylvania Dutch, hygienic spring house cleaning.

William Jay! Not the usual Billy. Sternly echoed from my mother as she honed to me like one of those Second World War straight line torpedoes.

Justice was swift.

Days later the prized desk was being pawed by Victor, the Slavic cabinet maker with the heavy, hair tufted hands and varnish stained nails.

Although days to complete, my sculpted creation disappeared beneath the 8,000 r.p.m. belt sander, a piece of original art history instantly transformed into sawdust. Is there no creative justice?

The blue clad knife now lived in the darkness of my father's locked metal box, perhaps never to dance on finished furniture again.

I never saw the knife again, never felt the comfortable worn smoothness of the blue case, never carefully thumbed the keen blade edge.

While recalling fond and sweet youth memories, I always include a brief visit to the cave of the Chippendale desk, collect my memories while smiling, and salute the knife wherever it may be.

ELWOOD'S CATAPULT

The deadly meteor almost evenly split the planet, a force violent enough to leave half the earth in a cooling sea of bubbling molten magna, the other half a now heavily enriched forested terrain, affording ideal living conditions for sophisticated man. These contrasting borders were formed by a continuous fire belching ring around the earth known as the deadly and impossible Pyrowall, a chasm perhaps one hundred yards across and maybe a quarter mile deep, an infinite pyrotechnic hell of unrecordable energetic heat. Absolutely impossible to cross, bridge or barely approach. The narrowest Pyrowall crossing point was home to Elwood and his two crudely constructed, flame scorched catapults.

Elwood C. Scaggs, twenty-one years ago, just before the catastrophic meteor explosion, was looked upon as a loner and too often cruelly bullied by his classmates. Overweight, the pudgy Elwood ate alone, quietly accepting the vicious teasing from the girls, even those lies about him eating paste and rolling his boogers. The caustic jokes continued through his school years and even bubbled over to his isolated job as chief strainer at the county's deteriorating sewerage treatment facility.

After work he methodically pointed the used Chevy four door toward his mother's cross town garage. Ricocheting from the sidewalk through the open windows and into the plush fabric of the headliner "Hey, smelly!" and "Are you looking for the circus?"

Squinting from the sun and holding back his tears, Elwood spotted the ill-mannered, street slick band through the partially fog discolored windshield. Each smirking face was registered by Elwood immediately and an express delivery of names and faces was made to those grey colored memory bank folds of the brain titled: Future Revenge. Actually, his file was quite thick and very detailed.

Keep in mind Elwood was understandably not a forgetful nor a forgiving person. Now, by God, things had dramatically changed; life had changed; people had changed; and, oh yes, Elwood had really changed.

Elwood's catapults were not just any catapults, but Elwood's tribute to the large rigs used by the Roman Empire and again during the fable enhanced religious crusades. Heavy hand hewn timbers, forged, hammer beaten, bolted steel connections with a twelve foot diameter racheted steel spoked wheel, cover braided winding cables, and individual or up to a family of five seating cups.

The catapults were effective but tempermental, subjected to ongoing red orange cinder showers, leaving the veil of ashen dusted landscape dotted with red embers that would occasionally burn through the cable sheathing. Erratic jettisons of first white, then orange to a final light blue flame spit from the very bottom of Devil's Canyon.

Near the jutting, scorched promontory that anchored the catapults, the orange hot canyon glowed at night; the soot blackened moon never shines here and an atmospheric, sherbert colored umbrella of light drifted miles above, cutting the dry, dead black sky.

Thin, glowing amber pinnacles rose from the Canyon's thermal floor with blue gas needle tips, each trailing a wire thin ribbon of cooling smoke, rippling like a swirling trail of bedroom incense.

Elwood slowly paced the fire rimmed promontory, his wrinkles layer caked with soot, ash and sweat. His hands and feet, heat cracked and stubble broken, were dressed in heat boils and partially peeled burn scars, highly contrasting the newly exposed pink skin and the dirt penetrated callouses. A dirty knotted head band clenched Elwood's singed and matted hair and the scorched loin cloth barely clad his sweat slickened torso.

Yeah, dirty job, and dangerous, "Yeah, but the only way to the other side and, yeah, who has the power now?" "Payback time!" he sneered as he spit on the hole punched steel catapult seat, watching the ball of phlemn do the griddle hop to nowhere.

Here they come, approaching from the cooler edge of the rim, the feinted smiles, the faked greetings as if long lost friends, the nervous back pats and then my turn. "Individual, couple, or family Canyon shots, no guarantees, weight limits apply, payments in diamonds or gold only."

Everyone knew the risk and failure rate of the catapult shot and somehow thought Elwood had some mysterious control over this acutely dangerous, high arched path of travel; and he certainly did.

Nineteen turns of the catapult's steel winding spool will splatter and explosion fry a normal sized man on the far Canyon wall, but twenty turns would chip him to the damp grassy knoll.

Elwood was king now, all your riches and all your fates were now in his hands.

He laughed away desperate sexual favors being offered by daughters and wives for an additional turn of the winding wheel as other hopefuls nervously offered additional dark velvet drawstring bags of cut and polished diamonds.

Finally, the lineup. "For some of you, it will take more diamonds for me to catapult your entire family across Devil's Canyon, and I can't guarantee that you heavy weight people won't get burned a little, at least a good singeing at the hands and feet. Sit on the shell, attach the leather belts with your kids on your lap and I'll yell when to close your eyes and mouth; remember, don't let cinders burn your eyes or pit scar your filmy lung tissue."

Too often the initial accelerating catapult thrust will pin the rider's internal organs against the shocked rib cage and spine, creating a washing machine sloshing of the stomach, liver, intestines and pancreas. Like liver colored, half filled water balloons, the organs accordion compress their abrupt retreat. These compressed organs expanding quickly from the white hot canyon heat tend to explode unpredictably under pressure.

A number of unfortunate's organs have exploded at the initial or completion arc of the journey, where the folks were closest to the rise of the explosive molten canyon heat. Sometimes only one membrane sack organ will explode at a time, usually the first high popping sound is the liver, the torn, thin sheened cordovan colored membrane quickly webs to vapor as it air fries in the heat. The now boiling liver bile fire crackers in all directions, frittering and crackling as the droplets evaporate. Other times all the organs go at once, kind of like the Saturday night jackpot of organ explosions. Something about the chemistry of those heated internal organ juices, when unexpectedly mixed, creates the most spectacular visuals. When the right stomach acids mix with the heated pancreatic juices, the explosion gives off evaporating blue green gas sparkles, ending in a veil of rising white hot ash. Some of the larger full organ blow out people, if high in the trajectory arch when exploding, provide elaborate peacock colored patterns of almost instantly evaporating organs.

Elwood remembered Mike, the good looking school star athlete, the guy that suggested he be used at the football practice tackling sessions. "It ain't funny now!" Well, can't remember just how many winding turns for Mike, too bad, now the memory of Mike is all in the green ring border of him, all his body fluids now fire dried on the far canyon wall, sort of like an over fried egg pattern, only crackling gel of body fat and a partial belt buckle remain. I told Mike five days ago that he had to slow down cause he was eleven pounds over the limit, him and that plump, chubby cheeked son of his, Timmy. Hell, the round kid exploded like a sticky, burning ball of fat just half way across, spraying exploding hot liver bile all over his sister.

Almost a struggle to get these folks saved today; they just won't listen. Years ago, when I first ran the catapults, it was popular to be thin and lightweight and I can't tell you how many times I've burned people until I got it down just right.

"How about you, you ready yet or do you want to wait and go early in the morning?"

LOS ANGELES LANDING

Downtown L.A. in early June with the sour scent of seedy Pershing Square widening my nostrils. The light blue, sunlit, rolling haze of unburned diesel fuel streaming behind the grease splattered street cleaner, leaving a trail of water brushed fluids of swirling spittle, vomit, untouchable wet clods of tissue and urine.

6:15 a.m. and downtown hardened beat cops make their first pass through the ragged shrubbery, methodically tapping each sleeping guest with their night sticks on their newspaper, mummy wrapped skulls. Staggering and cussing, the derelicts shuffle off to regroup in the sun below the central palm fountain.

A helluva long way from home, broke, standing in my only soiled clothes with a generous portion of fresh pigeon shit on my hair and right hand. Rinsing nature's deposit at the shared palm fountain, I noticed a greasy-windowed, 24 hour donut shop, mid-block on Garland Avenue.

The place was nearly empty as I gulped my courage and confronted the paper hatted counterman, a 30'ish, long side burned Mexican immigrant, clad with a cheaply plated gold crucifix necklace and two silver Navajo chipped turquoise rings.

I offered to sweep the place for three sugar donuts and a half pint of white milk. He agreed. Feinting my love for Mexico, we discussed his Yucatan home of Tulumex, and how he missed his sisters-sending cash to them every two weeks and visiting twice a year. He made more at the donut shop in one month than he could make in a year in Mexico. He knew broke and desperate when he saw it and pointed me toward the L.A. life survival on-ramp.

Guess I basically wanted to see the Pacific Ocean, magnetically, tractor beam drawn to the electric intrigue of sunny California. The wanderlust dream of every corn fed, mid western young man of eighteen years, three weeks.

Trying like hell to impossibly outrun the broken heartache of a two week old divorce: the I told you so result of a child marriage.

A week ago in a teenage alcoholic stupor, I climbed up on the Ohio Highway and hitchhiked to the Golden State, without a ticket, luggage, money, coat, or good sense: just me, the pain, and my pick a card, any card, future.

Nestor, the donut man, gave me a job lead, wincing while describing the work, as in very hot, very dirty, serious work: a brass foundry laborer in Eagle Rock, no questions or bull shit tolerated.

Following scribbled napkin directions, I boarded a bus full of Mexicans, the tubular overhead carriers bulged with string-bundled checkered ranch shirts, sealed one gallon plastic canisters of swaying sauces and peppers, wedged among masonry trowels, levels, and galvanized buckets of dry wall tools. Sure looked like this was the bus to serious work, with one wide eyed white boy without tools in the sixth seat.

Two blocks from the bus stop stood the foundry: a large, light yellow, corrugated metal building with circular, rusting roof ventilators streaming ribbons of distorted heat waves edged in light blue smoke.

The shrill whistle abruptly ended break time and at least forty hombres, busy smoking and propping the wall, quickly filed back through the roll up door under the watchful eye of the shop foreman, a middle aged Anglo in a sweat stained Dodger's hat. Most all the laborers look similar: folded head bandanas, crude, aging, adolescent drawn tatoos, tank tops filled with muscle, dirty, sweat soaked jeans and a challenging glint in their eye for the stray, out of context, white El Norte.

With my most puffed up posture I approached the lingering foreman. While inquiring about work, he eyeballed me top to bottom as I sold energy and my strong work effort as a team player.

The thin, obviously gay, Anglo in the small employment office scanned my one page work history application. Offering up a coy smile, he slowly explained that the work was hot, dirt, currently all Mexican, and dangerous. As he walked behind me, he cupped my right buttock then quickly withdrew like an octopus and in a feinted baritone voice boomed, "Start tomorrow as a form dye shaker, bring in an approved hard hat and protective goggles."

A job, income, food, clothes, a place to stay, all in my black sand grimed, Spanish dialect, smoking liquid brass, open pore future. Break your ass, silently pray for a stop in the production mold line, and lean into this sweat hog hard work.

With the leverage of a newly found job, my donut shop compadre gave me a well folded address of a hotel at Seventh and Garland. Nestor called from the sugar crusted donut shop phone to Habib, the hotel owner, verifying my new work and good guy character.

Not a palace, kind of like something from a bad horror film, the underlit, corner alley hotel was in sad need of repair. A single room, six story transient hotel, perched in the cross hairs of a neglect downtown core where street smarts are essential. Habib slipper shuffled to my second floor room, creaked the door and murmured, "Seven dollars a day, cash only, one key, you can buy your own deadbolt, no cooking fires, no fights, piss the mattress and it will cost you twelve dollars."

Home at last. A high paint peeled ceiling dangling a bare sixty watt bulb, faintly lighting the 8' x 12' room. Single leaking corner sink, a bring your own paper toilet and gang shower at the end of the hall. A large, single casement window, window and frames vacated years ago, now without glass only 1/4" wire mesh. A steel tube army cot with metal coil springs, one slightly stained 3" mattress, a coverless pillow and one wool army blanket.

The wood floor sloped to the door, largely covered by an ink-urine stained fake Persian carpet, heavily patterned with cigarette burns.

Gazing into the wall mounted discolored mirror above my single chair, I studied my face.

I'm here, got a job and a place to stay, now for that first time I'm gonna go see that ocean, and, Mom, if you could just see your boy now.

CYBORG LOVE

I used to think maybe one of every four or five hundred, but lately decided more like one for every thousand women. So intriguing and real like, deadly foreign cyborgs among us. You've seen 'em, hell we've all noticed some of their strange little giveaway traits of artificial intelligence, not human.

That rare moment when you snap your head to find one of them staring at you through a calibrated laser iris, their pupils electronically dilating as you are photo documented. You share the second glance just a little too long and there is a bolt of understanding: both sense the hunter and the prey, the human and the lab supplemented cyborg intelligence gathering female ranger.

You gotta admit, their bio tech engineers are incredible, can't tell machine from real, flesh from moisture backed rubber and, most importantly, intelligence and emotions, true or manufactured. Close up and personal, female emotions are co-mingled with computer data driven emotions from the human cyborg side.

Each alien ranger is unique: a great quiltwork of colorful, stamped circuitry parts blended with human flesh and organs, each a highly coordinated combination of the best, all cleverly set within the highest of social graces.

For slight fear, curiosity and verification, I slowly threaded my way through the oversized living room cocktail crowd, freshly scrubbed, like tuxedoed penguins, balancing oversized martini glasses on the flow of giggly chatter fueled by the alcoholic glow.

As I neared the ranger I couldn't help notice the effect of her presence, like an invisible silent cocoon of air about her, both dangerously magnetic and intriguing. She was stunning in the classic black cocktail dress, and, as I approached, I wondered which components were human or synthetic. She was instantly charming and conversational, unaware that I knew she was an alien cyborg. For a moment after her laughter, I saw a brief line of computer letters flash in intense green light just below her left eye: Batching Number 01228, Myra.

Myra was totally attractive and I instantly felt myself drawn to her, wanting to know more about this higher being from an afar planet.

While in the large granite clad guest bathroom, the door slowly opened and I stepped into the louvered linen closet upon first sight of Myra. Cramped and loudly breathing soap air from folded thick towels, she appeared through the louvered openings, standing there, eyes closed, before the full length mirror, remaining frozen as if to gather her thoughts.

Yep, she's one for sure, I thought, as she full body twitched, throwing her long synthetically woven raven hair over her back, completely revealing her computer key pad upper forehead, now a glow with minute green and blue flashing lights and scalloped shaped buttons. Her perfectly shaped lacquer hardened nails staccato tapped a series of keys as she updated her communications program. Then, like a freshman cheerleader, without hesitation she flipped into a hand stand, squarely in front of the open toilet stall, peeing perfectly into the toilet bowl, without raising the seat or missing a single drop.

Myra and I continued our relationship and it grew in a somewhat strange way. With a brief program adjustment on her hair camouflaged keyboard, she had access to all my personal and emotional concerns, always offering a response that was soothing and made me feel good.

Sure, some of our habits were very foreign and we performed most of them in private. Her parts exchange program was intrigue. She would sit limp and unconscious in the large padded armchair with her forehead keyboard removed while updating circuitry or the aggravating sounds of the pneumatic fed synthetic food paste and lubricants. On the other hand, she thought my facial shaving and deodorants were very comical and archaic.

Myra sensed the slightest suggestion of passion and her sexual arousal program was beyond fantasy. Our sweet and racy lovemaking was heightened by her ability to instantly expand or contract any of her body components at will.

We slowly and sweetly confessed our love and denied the impossibilities of a human cyborg life together. Now we are to be blessed with our first offspring and the challenges are more than a few. Each evening, Myra and I consider the appropriate accommodations of real and synthetic portions of our future son. Although not yet complete, we have decided on several. His emotions shall be human with all behavioral characteristics such as anger, greed and jealousy removed. Instead, alien circuitry for peace, compassion and understanding will be substituted. All physical attributes will be synthetically enhanced and our junior will always walk without pain, never show signs of aging and we promise he will stay away from your daughter.

WOODY

The tightly wound Black Diamond steel guitar strings of the Gibson, model D-28, knew they were being accurately plucked by an experienced right hand, one that tickled and pulled the rich, throaty tones from the finely crafted instrument, so yearned for by amateur musicians. Crispy harmonics reverberated through the human rib cage while the worn, polished steel finger picks delivered everything from classic ballads to the Appalachian strains of "Fire on the Mountain" and "Wildwood Flower", all executed in perfect harmony without ever missing a lick. Yep, John Woodrow, or Woody, knew 'em all and was a damn fine steel string flat picker, a too rare undocumented human tribute to mountain music. The guitar was a part of Woody's life; like an extra anatomical appendage, they never separated.

In order to support his ever constant music addiction, Woody passed himself off as a university student: scheduling the minimum number of classes, requiring just enough effort to qualify his student loans and side step the horrid thoughts of a full time job. For Woody, eleven years of strung out Art History and Music Appreciation courses resulted in a rather peculiar combination; a guitarist that with too many drinks would awkwardly blend mountain ballad lore with the likes of Paolo Ucello and other Renaissance painters.

We appreciated one another and wove a friendship of music, art history, laughter, killer weed, bull shit, and double shots of tequila with beer chasers. I graduated and left for Europe, leaving Woody in the smoky back room of the Union Bar and Grill with his guitar in hand and three brim filled double shots by the grey smudged glass ash tray.

Years slipped away and after Europe, the Army, marriage and a thousand other lives, I sought him out: same house by the Hocking River, same Woody, same hair with a dab of grey, same left hand, calloused finger tips from the steel strings and the same heat for music.

Guitar case in hand, he greeted me with a loud "Rug head!" the nick name he insisted captured my curly hair. He now had a part time job, just enough to buy guitar strings, bologna white bread sandwiches, white wine and cover dog food and river cabin rent. Four days a week he played for inmates of the large mental health asylum, an early 1900s red masonry cluster of buildings cradled in the soft hard wooded hills of the plush green southern Ohio valley.

I accompanied him to his work and he agreed to give me the full tour, assuring me with a wink that we would not be visiting the D wing but telling me some of the inmates were crazy as shit house rats. This was an understatement by any standards verified by a scar on his forehead, delivered last year by an elderly, frail appearing grandma type that surprisingly clobbered him with a steel tray when he refused to play Red River Valley a fourth time.

Before entering the electrically controlled main gate, we sat on a manicured knoll where trustees were permitted to freely roam, clad in the standard identifiable denim and for the most part looking and acting just like you and me. As we sat outstretched,

Woody tuned his guitar and I wondered what was next; my wonderment was soon answered.

Over the rise of the knoll, head down and wet nose sniffing, a beagle pup cut a zig zag pattern in the soft grass, leaving stitch like footprints too numerous to count and heading our way, determined as tracking a rabbit. Closely behind followed three female residents, each with white linen skull caps, compressing only the tops of their unkept tormented hair. Longer strands were unconsciously knotted, pulled and frayed by their dirty, broken finger nailed ever roaming fingers. Each inmate carried a short branch from the nearby maple and oak droppings. The women diligently followed the erratic dog trail while frustratingly stabbing at each paw mark with their sticks. Unable to pace the puppy, they agonized over unattended prints while scampering like bobbing corks. As each wild eyed matron passed in line, they momentarily paused by us, locked their gaze and shrieked, "Ain't it a shame, ain't it a shame!" then disappeared over the next knoll.

Shortly thereafter, a middle aged denim clad man approached, the one I earlier noticed peeking from behind a mature oak. He casually ambled our way with stiffened arms, hands deeply in his jean pockets. Stopping directly in front of me he paused, licked his chapped lips, then very slowly pulled his right hand from his jeans. Unlocking his fist in slow motion, his extended palm revealed a sweat soaked, stained Camel cigarette butt, his prized sole possession. Abruptly clam shelling shut his hand, he asked for a match and I offered a clip of matches. Upon seeing them he instantly plucked them from me, rapidly retreating several steps, he held the match pack high above his head screaming, "See these, I'm keeping these!", clinched the pack in his front teeth and ran.

Woody and I mused if we might hear fire department sirens that night.

As Woody played for the various wards of heavily medicated unfortunates that afternoon, I witnessed the common threads of mental illness that could randomly select any of us, silently, without warning, and end our most prized possession, sanity.

Interrupted sleep patterns, babbling, rage, tears, tormented dreams, self destruction, loveless hours, fears and phobias, over medicated depression, loss of direction, family, lovers, integrity, esteem and self respect, monitored non privacy, bland institutional food without sharp silverware, the ever present scent of urine and all outside light and views framed by steel bar lattice work. God Bless our sanity, brother! Please don't let the roulette crazy wheel stop on my number.

Andy, a life long inmate of C ward, excitedly introduced himself as a sculptor of man, effusing his artistic excitement. When told I was an architect, he relished the idea that we probably shared creative talents and celebrated immediately by pre soaking his trousers while offering a hand shake by extending his right hand, a hand suspiciously sienna stained with dark brown moon shaped crescents rimming each finger nail. Andy whispered a private invitation to view his prized sculptures and beckoned me to his steel framed bunkbed.

Slowly pulling back the thin, urine stained blue striped mattress, the steel angle of the bed frame housed his gallery, a dozen or so tiny hand rolled people figures, each primitive figure a half inch or so in length, each with a main body, attached legs, arms and little round ball shaped heads with indented eyes, some hard, some soft but all of them lovingly molded from genuine Andy shit.

Later that evening I bid goodbye to Woody and thoughts of the institution, wondering if someday I might unfortunately step over the delicate brain line and hoping that Woody would be there to play for me.

DARK NURSERY

I diligently serve as an apostle of eternal evil, delivering the absolute assurance that many living warm blood humans will pass briefly through this life into the forever wickedness of blackness, never ending suffering and merciless pain. I am the chill of death uninvitedly moving cat like to your death bed, the anti-Christ, the real king of darkness. Know this, for many of you selected to receive the mark: there is no after life except pure evil.

I walk among all of you, appearing as a commoner, acting as you, yet you would never realize what lies camouflaged just behind this thin skin. At my choosing you are all mine, forever; when our eyes meet, do you really know that I am looking deeply into your spirit. For that split second you may hesitate with a small gasp, but by then it is far too late; I control your soul for now and forever. You have passed through the jagged thin crack of life to the hereafter, made the mortal transfer journey and are now forever mine. Forget the bright light at the end of the life tunnel, discard the framed snapshots of your mortal life, feed me all your soul, submit to your master.

You shall do as I say and embrace the wickedness of blackness; for after my visitation, there is no after life for you except pure evil.

Two acknowledged methods of delivering satanic evil to warm bloods are most common; the brief but intense searing eye contact, locking the warm blood in place while transmitting merciless suffering and the marking on the forehead of a pentacle star with the nail tip of the index finger.

Eleanor Rosenthal, 68 years old, widow, wealthy, educated, good Central Park Avenue address, Suite 6B. Slipping by the doorman, I posed as a package delivery man while fondling the box addressed to her.

After twice tapping on her decorative door, she reluctantly released two steel deadbolts and unlatched the door, peering owl like through the three inch opening secured by the brass safety chain. Our eyes instantly met and she knew the searing glow of evil; unable to unlock her gaze, she abruptly inhaled quickly retreating two steps. By then the black act was completed. She was forever marked and I silently left by the stairs, leaving my brown paper wrapped package at her door, a pair of new black shoes, appropriate for her coming funeral.

Douglas Peter Cummins, two days old, white male Caucasian, St. Peters Hospital, second level nursery wing. Shadowed behind the teddy bear print, pleated drapes of the hospital nursery, I moved among the infant bassinets during the early morning hour, halting at the laminated identification card: Cummins, P., male, seven pounds, twelve ounces. Soft, uninterrupted deep sleep, cooing baby breath.

Straightening my cold, bony index finger, I lightly traced a star on the smooth warm forehead. For a split second the new born flinched and gurgled, then returned to innocent blissful sleep. No matter now, the mark of evil has already shadow-blackened the infant's heart.

My quota today for death card dealing totals nine; with two markings completed I quicken the pace by using the intense eye method exclusively. It is so efficiently effective with all unsuspecting warm bloods.

The man at the bus stop, the office secretary in the elevator, the market cashier and that initially outspoken teenager near the bike rack, all gave way to the unstoppable magnetic power of the piercing evil glare, yielding to the eternal black force.

Souls have been emptied today, hope and faith have given way to crushed dreams; mercy and joy are forever choked by pain and hopelessness and several warm bloods have been forever tattooed and branded with the veined black blood of evil.

By the way, have you noticed the intense staring of a stranger lately?

INSIDE RAILROAD

Pay close attention please. Put on the complete sanitary suit, including boots and visor, and we'll enter the brain cavity through the cerebral cord. Remember, don't touch anything, no cameras please, and stay on the designated trail. Note how the millions of brain trails at the top here are red and turn to blue at the lower levels. The upper, or red hot brain thought trails, handle all the emotional stuff: love, hate, compassion, anger and jealousy.

See that curve ahead with all the red tangled damage: the guy's wife left him and his emotions came runnin' up through here at warp speed, never made the curve. Now, weeks of brain wave repair and realignment will be required at that heart break intersection. Strange though, every now and then, after the divorce when he would have too many whiskeys by himself, he would blind stagger down memory lane and the heart breaking waves would come around that red hot curve and jump the track. Serious damage, it happened every couple of weeks or so for several years.

Matters of the heart seem to do the most track damage. Hell, near his birthdays and holidays we would order sections of track in advance of his tail spinning love tantrums. His brain and his heart seem to have some sad disconnect: the brain would always send a load of the reality love stuff that would directly collide when his foolish heart dangerously climbed onto the track.

Lower on the left, a jealous rage brain wave collided with a set of mellow compassion waves and is still smoldering. The compassion waves were severely damaged.

The blue colored brain trails handle all the rudimentary life learning tasks and the difficulties are well documented by all the nicks and gouges in the track edges. That wrinkled section there happened while learning how to tie your own shoes and memorizing those stupid multiplication tables, especially eleven times twelve. The bent track happened when the fifth grade boys and girls squared off shoeless in the maple floored gymnasium to learn the two step.

The first automobile accident, toothaches, public diarrhea, playground fist fights, memorizing organic chemistry formulas and army general orders, the capital of Madagascar and income averaging tax forms all took their toll. All that blue grey information so vital and worthless. Never once have we used integrated calculus at the grocery check out line.

Most of the blue brain trails haven't been traveled in years; yet they still work and those spiral bends are the results of all the dirty jokes we shared after Sunday School.

Several of you during the tour have asked about that shining silver track near the center there, the slightly dusty one without any scratches. Never been used, runs from here straight up through the trap door in the top of the skull, nobody really knows where it goes from there. We keep it in A-1 condition, always ready but never know when it will be used.

It's the death track, the final mental run, the last brain wave journey, you know, when the grasping death bed thoughts are quickly getting religion and the dimming lights at the boarding station are surrounded in the thinly veiled chill of death. All aboard, brain track D-1, one way only, no return trip, no baggage required and all destinations are final.

By the way, we have no replacement parts or track for the death run.

ALBERT THE TOAD

Albert the toad, thank you, not to be confused with our water loving cousins, frogs, We are a long line of Hawaiian cane toads, basic land lovers with a penchant for juicy bugs and the exceptional night life, only a toad can live. Personally, I am two years old and have well developed characteristics common to my eleven brothers and sisters: those glassy bulging dark eyes, large toes and tissue thin foot webbing, an excessively baggy drapery of mottled dark brown skin and, of course, the warts. Everybody knows about the well rumored toad warts.

My grandfather's father would gather the toad clan together on moonlit nights and croak the toad wisdom to the younger hoppers, toad rules of the road so to say. What bugs were sweet or bitter, how to negotiate with centipedes, finding water and generally acceptable social toad protocol. Life was mellow then, 3 a.m. moonlit croaking contests, distance peeing competition and connect the wart games.

We were more of a family then, the cane fields were our home and island developers were unheard of. First those big scary yellow bulldozers, followed by the roads and trucks, trucks with ballooned murderous tires that can pancake you in a heartbeat.

My father remembers seeing the first electrical residential night light and how the clan first thought a piece of the moon had fallen.

Slow hopping closer at 4 a.m. we ogled the foreign looking house. What a very strange contraption this was all solid with only a few openings although the opening at the bottom of the one garage door was accessible to us 2-1/2" high toads. We all hopped home, pausing to croak our opinions and sternly warned by grandfather never to enter the strange humans garage. As we croaked and bellowed the night away, as good toads always do, I kept wondering about the hidden mysteries of the garage.

Against all toad wisdom, I escape-hopped one Wednesday morning at 3 a.m. to the front of the garage. The small bottom opening fell black under the shower of moonlight and I nervously hopped inside: very dark hard concrete and two vehicles with those killer tires, a number of shelves with very strange items and workbench, tough to see with the only crack of light from beneath the door into the house. I hopped and sniffed all about, inspecting the underside of the vehicles, sniffing the broom and mop then visiting all the wooden handled garden tools. While sizing up a hole at the base of the work bench, my heart stopped and I relieved myself on the garage floor as nervous toads often do.

The lighthouse like beam of white flooded me as the house door quickly opened, profiling a large man that snapped on the bright overhead fluorescent lights, freezing my movements mid hop. As the monstrously tall man moved toward me, I power sprang to the small hole in the base, thrusting my body sideways, finding myself very uncomfortably wedged in a small dead end recess with little wiggle room.

As I squirmed, mortified, my toad heart sank as a huge head appeared near the floor line and a flashlight beam flooded my cramped surroundings. Then the very worst of dreams: the man pushed a rag tightly into the opening and all went black. Grandpa toad was right: here I was, trapped in a tight crypt, stuck on my side with no light and little air.

You bet I was scared, small glistening beads of toad sweat on my folded webbed feet and beginning to constantly blink, as nervous toads do. I repeated my toad prayers, slowly croaking the wish to be free again deep in the damp thickets of the silent moon washed cane.

Hours later the rag was removed and air and light drenched my aching body. Sensing daytime silence, I squirmed free and noticed a freshly cut wood block, a likely permanent replacement for the rag. I double quick hopped out the door and rejoined the clan as the luckiest toad on the island.

Weeks later, I returned to the forbidden garage, again inspected the tires and the scary hole at the work bench base, now sealed with a tightly fitted wood block. That giant-like man cut me a break, he gave me my escape opportunity, a true humanitarian, or perhaps he just realized his next lifetime as a possible toad. Gratefully exiting I left two droppings in the center of the garage to signal my departure.

Now, in lifelong gratitude, the clan assembles in his landscaped flower bed each full moon and we croak our toad serenades.

WE BE ROCKIN'

Armed with a truck load of illegal habits and a thimble full of cures, I eye contacted each of the band members with that final glossy eyed look of understanding, that private piercing look that says, "We're ready, let's rock!"

Things started innocently enough: home alone with the radio up, me playing air guitar in front of my sister's dressing room mirror, never missing a lick or single gyration, I wanted it!

My first electric Stratocaster guitar, a Fender bass and we wuz launched as a noisy, neighborhood garage band. Since then everything has been an accelerating upward progression: promiscuous girlfriend to nude hotel groupies, band sleeping in a small moody tour van to limos and private jets, on the road bologna sandwiches to lobster and champagne, overdrawn bank accounts to investment counsel briefings, marijuana to heroine, Chevrolet van to Ferrari Boxer and finally, her to them.

The climb to the top was on jagged glass, some experiences leaving deep scars that galvanized us into a crazy whirling comraderie of self loving musicians.

Lead singer and guitarist, drummer, rhythm guitarist, keyboard, back up vocalists, all expertly supported by the best sound engineers and eccentric electrical technicians available, a spacey cluster of light and sound fanatics, identifiable only in head phone sets, accompanied by a contingency of sunglassed, black shirted, over muscled security gorillas. What a traveling family: from city to city, concert to concert, modern gypsies camp to camp, rock on! It's in the blood.

The band members are a patchwork of back alley style and eccentric self adornment, a pumping, sweaty mass of long hair, leather, chains and bright silk microphone scarves, all infilled with a cheap side show variety of body tattoos. We traveled, performed, played and sometimes slept in our corporate head turning stage garb, outfitted for instant on the spot fun - anytime, anywhere!

From the final practice, green padded sound room to center stage was always a swaggering reality check journey, your momentary final thoughts before feeling the totally swallowing, soon to be released, energy of two hundred thousand rock fans.

Deafening applause, blinding spot lights, our opening number and the entire crowd is on their feet. The freight train energy of the band is harmonically synchronized. My rib cage and body move with the anticipation of each note. I'm SuperGlue bonded to the rhythm, tight as shadow dancing and stuck together like dots on the dice. My heart expands and there it is, the magic moment, everyone dancing, smiling illegal smiles and rockin!

LOVE STUFF

Oh yea, oh yes, the stuff we do for love, life stuff, romantic stuff, all that stuff we did, do now, and will do tomorrow to satisfy our unpredictably hungry love beast.

You and me, well, we've done some painful, funny, heartbreakin' stunts to get where we are; fact is, everyone participates with being the love fool every now and then.

Matters of the heart, the very stuff that butter-fattens the net incomes of the mental health therapy swarm. Take my class, take this course, breathe deeply and write me a check. We'll have your heartache fixed during our next fifteen, pay in advance, installment sessions.

Naw, the heart lessons are only learned by experiences; you know those thin cracks that found our hearts when we were feeling so Southern blue love sick, the 4 a.m. tears in the dark kind of pain.

Endless hours, hygienically priming the love nest, readying every sequenced detail to guarantee a score. Early Saturday on hands and knees polishing furniture and hardwood floors, trips to the Deli and fish market, chilled champagne and white wine, shrimp cocktails, fresh flowers, mood lighting and music at the touch. The love trap is now officially cocked and open for business.

Remember the last time someone stood you up? Met her in a city bar late last Wednesday night, telephone number on a crumpled napkin on my dresser by the pile of bar change. Dinner date, meet for cocktails at 7:30. Prompt at 7:20, I order an Irish whiskey with water back from the corner table. 7:45 then 8:00. I reorder and leave at 8:30 with that feeling. Love trap set at home, all dressed up and no place to go; mercy, I'll take my love matters to the street tonight.

Stubby young hands, awkwardly cut red paper Valentine hearts on the dotted lines. The annual assembling of the grammar school Valentine's Day box, a highly decorated shoe box with a slot cut into the lid to receive all those doilied, red hearted greetings from my favorite girl friends. Just got a dinky little signed heart from Charlene, my fourth grade heart throb, and I gave her my largest store bought card, signed Love, Billy.

Love by gifts at Christmas to the current adolescent pursuit. A white leather trimmed music jewel box inhaled all my paper route cash. I spent hours designer wrapping the box in shiny paper and bows, placing the love card just below the green and blue ribbon. Hand delivered by yours truly through the early Christmas morning snow, I clumsily handed the gift to her surprised mother at their door and about faced toward home. She called two days later; sounding cool and distant, she said her mother thought the gift was too mature for a fifth grader and it would be returned. Oh, this Saturday? Oh, yeh, well how aboutFriday? Oh, you are? Well, I'll call you sometime.

And who could forget the mother of all social inventions, the Senior Prom. Privately engineered prom parties, a weekend of madness, an exclamation point in our lives with rented tuxedos, spit shined shoes, corsage, folding money of unfamiliar presidents and a half pint of Jack Daniels in my inside lapel pocket. Armed with the family Chrysler hard top, I ritualized the always uncomfortable parental introductions and unkeepable promises, whisping their knock-out daughter into the night. The weekend, an historic and hysteric romantic marathon.

Well, now that we are all mature and well experienced with all matters of the heart, we need not fear being the sometimes love fool, or do you ever feel that the love trap door you are now standing on could swing open without warning?

DISAPPEARING VILLAGE

The remote sea edge delivered endless tapered waves of international culture to the ever absorbing beach. Receding wavelets deposited flotsam, bubbled necklaces, linking all that touch and share the sea.

The sea knows and silently witnesses everything, birth in the Mediterranean, death in the Black Sea, love on the Aegean, New York Harbor bars and floating dead dogs in the China Sea. Bobbing frost whiskered Arctic seal pups and paint brush splattered tropical parrots all lace our salty, blue, hydrogen oxygen continental bond.

After two pleasantly relaxing shallow dives, I sprawled belly down on the straw mat that smelled slightly like China. The sizzling sun slowly transformed water droplets to ashen salt stains on my back and forearms as I faintly scented the warming skin of my wrist.

As the trapped tepid sea water drained from my right ear I abstractly raked the beach with my water wrinkled hands. My anticipating finger pads met a polished stone, smooth to the touch and perfectly formed in a Latin cross plan, a rare prize comfortably cradled in my moist palm.

This was no regular stone; this geometry was carefully crafted by others.

Clasping the intriguing talisman, I again slipped below the water line for a final sub sea level excursion, this time closer to the outer reef shelf.

Drifting with the grace of slow moving sea weed the ocean descent led to an unexpected jutting sandbar shelf well secluded and parentally protected by the cantilevered reef canopy of pocked calcium.

Momentarily captured bright laser sun rays revealed an entire miniature subterranean city complete with crystalline fairy land turrets and spires fragile as sun bleached bird bones and delicate as fine thin porcelain English china.

Features included sugar cube scaled houses and grander accommodations showcasing buttresses, double arches and ornament laden facades with the classic underwater swim through window.

A veil of gauze-thin diamond sand twinkled back the water shimmering outline of this long deserted micro culture like so many 4th of July sparklers. The central plaza of this tiny wonderment was grandly detailed: curved spires, coliseum seating, clearly the magnetic spiritual hub of a once thriving culture. The pleasing geometric plaza floor, worn smooth by many lifetimes, was complete except the missing cross shaped keystone at the plaza center.

As I was marvelously suspended by the sleepy warm currents, my effortless body derigibled above the shell of this community.

Surreally in the delicate arms of the soothing sea, all body functions except breathing on hold, it hit me! The discovered cross shaped stone in my right hand is the missing plaza key stone.

Like a sleepy Koi, I gingerly descended to the plaza floor in slow motion. I carefully aligned the missing piece; and, upon contact, the stone snugly slotted to its abandoned home.

Within moments, a bright strobe blue arch bathed the village in all its final documented form.

Then sadly, but unstoppably, it began. Like small trickling erosion, the village began to crumble: first the spires and turrets, now mishapened like toppling court jester hats, followed by arches dominoing into collapsing buttresses.

With the sureness of hour glass sand the once stately city slowly saluted gravity and again became woven into the level silent ocean floor.

HARD SCRABBLE

In the grip of the hardscrabble, blunt edge of Detroit's lower west side, it was Friday night at the end of the month, days before payday and welfare check arrival five days out. No money and desperate. The west side poverty belt of monotonous, four level walk-up masonry flats with graffiti and soup stained walls and a stubble of rooted landscape, peppered with cigarette butts, condoms, candy foil and discarded wads of gum with crooked teeth marks.

Each building accordion bulged with people of color, unfortunately broke, addicted, half hungry and well beyond the pride of money issues.

The sloping, asphalt-patched, basketball court by building number six was ground zero for the neighborhood buzz, and a necessary stage backdrop for all the constant exchanges of drugs, street stories, money, brown bag alcohol, and prostitution. You might say it was the trade route intersection of all local goings on, both good and evil. It was also where Gino Carlotti parked his mobile unit near month's end.

Thousands of General Motor's production line shift workers were let go four years ago, discontinuing the body stamping plant left most all west side families quickly without money and means to keep utilities on and feed their families. Their only serious alternative was a visit with Gino on a cash basis.

The once proud economy and model welfare state eroded to a new low of government mistrust and collapse of the monetary system. The country quickly attention-stepped into two very distinct long lines: those with money and those without.

The wealthy influenced local government rewrote certain By-Laws to serve their accelerating fancies, such - as initiating the Cash For Fingers Program for poverty impacted families. Some say the bill smacked of special interests, lobbied on behalf of the Food Export Union; others say the board members simply loved munching on fingers. Either way, it permitted the public sale and extraction of fingers by a licensed remover, including minors.

Curbside, along the pock-marked ghetto streets was a predictable, lopsided palette of the young, old, and misshapen, excepting the many doe-eyed children, the quieter ones with fewer or no fingers. Some left only with the stump of a hand and a single thumb, some healed, and others with tell-tale crimson stained bandages.

The Fingers For Money Program changed the nature of young and adolescent pursuits. No longer were piano and guitar lessons offered, lack of small fingers also limited basketball and football enthusiasm, giving way to games of soccer and kick the can.

Saddened parents reluctantly decided to visit Gino as a last resort to stem emergency medical bills and cover food costs for cheap casseroles and thin soups. Moms and dads solemnly discussed the digital sacrifices with their young, telling them this was for the family and many of their young friends had already made contributions. Little boys and girls cringed and stammered with the prospect, some even cried while inspecting and rubbing their small hands together.

Gino offered cold, hard cash for fresh fingers; the going rate brought one thousand dollars for an index and seven hundred dollars for any other full length finger. Matched index fingers taken at the same cutting, netted a two hundred fifty dollar bonus.

No racial inequities here: Hispanic, Afro-American, Puerto Rican, Anglo, Asian, and Indian, all God's little children's fingers fetched the same price.

Gino Carlotti, a paunch, Italian misplaced New Yorker, loved children; but business was business for himself and his brothers. He only worked the last week of each month, operating the traveling finger wacking machine. Curling his thick mustache upward, he thought of himself and his business as soothing and beneficial to the neighborhood's needs. Was he not more than fair to the nervous parents, and calm and reassuring to the tearful, trembling children?

All prepared in rubber apron, he set out across town toward the west side ghetto parking lot by the basketball court.

His radically converted Bookmobile was the perfect functional response to his business of traveling finger wacking with a child friendly exterior and a very functional operative-like, wash-down stainless steel, windowless interior.

Gino flipped the yellow toggle switch in the driver's cab and adjusted the volume of Mary Had a Little Lamb at sixty decibels through the exterior speakers with a volume control by the processing equipment to mask the children's first, shrill screams.

Faintly heard from blocks away, Gino's mobile finger wacker. The ghetto, at first straining for confirmation, silently stiffening as the musical rhyme slowly became louder, until, finally, around the 181st Street corner rolled Gino.

The repainted Bookmobile was artfully air brushed with children story characters and friendly barnyard animals. The only business exterior giveaway was the thin, black rubber-ringed, finger insert holes along the curbside of the vehicle. Each right and left hand series set at different heights to accommodate toddlers as well as adolescents. With this set up, a youngster could put in just one, two, three or all of his fingers at once for the bonus prize. Once inserted, however, fingers were caught in a Chinese like finger puzzle and could not be withdrawn.

The interior of the vehicle housed a sleek, semi-automated, finger processing production line, from initial wacking to final vacuum packing for sale or export.

Clad in rubber boots and apron, Gino lowered his blood splattered, clear, plexiglas face mask as he finally inspected the various colors and shapes of nine squirming fingers protruding inside his vehicle. He turned up the volume and hit the red slicer button. The pneumatic, razor-edged bar blade tracked vertically, instantly providing a small shower of blood-spurting fingers, ricocheting and bouncing into the nail pulling drum strainer, then length sorted, onto par boiling, skinning, seasoning to taste and packing.

The market for kid's fingers has rapidly expanded as an international delicacy. Restaurants and gift-packed orders are soaring and Third World Countries are being scoped as finger harvesting areas of opportunity. Gino and his brothers, Rico and Alberto, prepare their export quotas. Their most popular item is the eight pack: a twelve ounce, vacuum packed, glass holiday jar with a mix of three index and eight middle and ring fingers with special spices, guaranteed free of any fingernails or bone clippings. Tins containing two to twenty-four fingers in party pack combinations are also available.

Tonight was special: as promised for months, Gino brought the new, shining, aluminum alloy mountain bike. Unobtainable for all ghetto children, it would be a bonus for anyone offering the complete set of eight matched fingers, plus, the matched index finger bonus money.

Children and parents assembled solemnly by Gino's vehicle and brief conversations were whispered among Gino and parents. Deals were cut and fingers soon would be.

Disappearing into the vehicle, the volume suddenly increased and parents prison-shuffled their wide eyed, crying children to the black ringed finger holes. Parents urged, "Do it for Daddy, sweetie," and "It won't hurt, Jimmy did it and didn't even cry."

Jasmine, a quiet pretty mulatto nine year old Puerto Rican, clung to her mother with her eyes tightly closed. Juan Paul, her father, desperately needed the stomach surgery or he would die.

Without prompting, Jasmine opened her wet eyes, quickly stepped to the black ringed holes and dedicated all eight fingers. Collapsing, she was given an injection for shock, bandaged, and cradled by her grateful parents.

Gino slowly wheeled the bonus prize to Jasmine. Unable to ever grasp the handle bars, she might be able to sell the bicycle for food or winter heat.

Personally, freshly clipped fingers are always the best; but, after all, it is an acquired taste. Nothing like a dry Chardonnay with a pile of broiled fingers served on a garnished bed of pasta.

Here, try one, finger lickin' good, ain't it? Just spit any bones in this bowl.

SKIN DEEP

I could easily wack her at this distance, one serious, horizontal thrust of my calloused five foot tail would rocket twelve feet of very well experienced, attitude dripping, bull alligator up and onto the blue tile edge of the boat dock.

Another southern posh Bayou country club summer regatta dance. Just before midnight she stepped away from the polished, maple parquet patterned dance floor, feeling the warm Bayou thickness of the dead still night embrace her, close as mummy wrappings.

Cicadas and bull frogs pumped out the sweet, swamp scented, two note Creole harmony.

She whiskey leaned on a fluted Georgia column near the boat house bar, finally unleashing her dance commanding, strapped, tortured feet from the cruel Italian red leather spikes. Left hand dangling shoes, right hand choking a bourbon on the rocks as the damp dock surface cooly smothered her raging foot fires.

The early morning veil of swamp fog lazily rose, like uncurling gauze from the unending black glass-polished, backwater.

Just below the brackish water surface, my unhooded eyes scoped a moving figure in a black sequined cocktail dress with several diamond accessory glitters.

Distorted by water, yet outlined against the inky night by the far off sodium vapor lamp, she swayed at the dock edge, transfixed, gazing into the black gold as if to seek life's southern female mysteries.

I could hair trigger rise from this unsuspecting pool, thrashing with bone snapping, organ puncturing death, snap clutching your hips and upper legs between misshaped, double rows of bacteria crusted, razor sharp teeth. Force crushing your mid section, pulled back into the water, then spiral rolled to the bottom, drowning, while I continually side tear and regrip with my jaw, securing you under a log or a mangrove bank. Kind of like stashing you in the refrigerator for later.

Could'a taken her, but I was really called in for bigger game even though I did kinda want to know if she was tasty. It's all gonna happen next weekend at the National Leather Accessory Annual Convention and Boat Regatta. I'm hoping to score Angelo Capinetto, the president, for the future of all the up-coming young bull gators and their eggs.

Years ago I had squinted at the gator skin loafers, gator hide belts and purses, future life as a wallet or accessory meant retailer-gator wars and according to my scars and puncture wounds, "I'm da baddest gator in da Bayou".

Angelo Capinetto always looked like an untethered, Las Vegas cash car dealer, with those lavish, border line theatrical accessories, oversized diamond ring, jeweled cuff links and that obnoxious diamond crusted, horseshoe shaped lapel stick pin. Middle aged, New York Italian with paunch, Angelo dabbed forehead perspiration with his lightly starched dinner napkin. "These southern states are just too damn hot for these meetings."

He excused himself as the after dinner cigar and brandy ritual began.

Another great profit year for genuine alligator skin accessories and the new line of women's gator thongs and hide hats all sound promising.

The heel click of Angelo's hand stitched gator loafers slowed as he aimlessly strolled the boat dock landing. Galvanized pontoons floated the boarding pad just inches above the late evening water line. Peering silently into the heavy, blanket-covered Bayou darkness, Angelo paused, loosened his alligator belt and passionately lit the damp, broad green leafed, hand rolled Cuban cigar. Finally, relaxed eyes closed, he exhaled, unknowingly poised for swift and deadly Bayou justice.

This time, head partially surfaced in a tuft of floating brush, I edged, ever so slowly towards the dock, no surface movement or air bubbles, a patience practiced, tail powered drift; I'm within three feet and he senses nothing.

Dark Italian features, shiny raven hair, thick stubby fingers, quite a sizeable guy in that tailor made blue suit and open collar silk shirt. The occasional red glow of his cigar served as my fatal honing target.

Explosively breeching upward with my salivating, cotton colored jaw fully extended, I hit Angelo at the lower chest line, ripping through his stomach and crushing his rib cage. Snap clamping his head and shoulders, we writhed one loop below the water line.

Angelo was very dead before we attended to our very special business at the Bayou bottom. As agile as a gator can be, I claw peeled several patches of Angelo's unpunctured skin from his bloating body. These carefully claw folded, amber and white,

Italian skin packs were ritualistically presented to the larger bull gator families. As was the long standing swamp gator tradition, female gators would now sow Angelo's skin pieces into carrying bags for female gators, friendship bands for male gators and nest egg liners.

MOUNTAIN FOLK

Not that long ago, before our computer friends could slyly profile newly found groups of just discovered bushmen in New Guinea, another society on the opposite end of the globe in misty mountain Appalachia was evolving. Both groups faced ultimate and unavoidable destruction as neighboring societies thumped with the successes and excesses of a more finely-filed sophisticated civilization.

A proud group that lived by their wits, mule stubborn with the salivating determination of a lip curled pit bull. A pure test tube full of Americana rock-a-billy subculture unique and diverse as jazz.

Louisiana toward the Carolinas, southern Kentucky, Tennessee, Alabama and Mississippi, combinations of ranch cowboys and mountain people, all part of the chicken fried steak and grit belt, fix your car in the front yard territory, Bible thumpin, inter-marryin, trailer livin, tooth-neglected hill people. The heart throb of unfortunate circumstances mirrored through each inbred generation of uneducated, stubborn-proud, American Hill Billies, the proud gypsies of the South. These close clan inter- arguing, sometimes lop sided families, specialize too often in large numbers tempted by a generation passed-on art of sometimes food stamp forgery and welfare fraud.

All mountain people are significantly afflicted by the money disease, as in never enough to go around and what's going around is going to the wrong places. Money for most mountain people wouldn't stay in the sweaty palm of their right hand any longer than it could stay put in a snap down pocket. All Presidents printed on paper currency are allergic to leather wallets in this part of the world, and under no circumstances will Franklin, Grant, Jefferson and Lincoln stay in any mountain wallet fold, only Washington, and then only occasionally.

It's all part of the mountain people's life trials, the cards they've been dealt, the Allen Greenspan status checked and initialed at the bottom left of the page referencing "those fiscally unable to sustain the low medium standard of living necessary for basic existence."

There's always been some sort of invisible shield between mountain people and city folks, a cultural hinged screen door between Marlboros and hand rolled Bull Durham, rib eye steak and fried boloney, BMW coupe and trashed Ford pick up, a professional couple with children and a non-working couple with four kids, a two bedroom, two bath, hardwood floor Brownstone and a forty foot house trailer with a tarp covered lean-to wood shed.

Shorty's silver amalgamed front tooth replacement gleamed in the smoke filled glow of the '65 Mustang coupe dome light. Just enough light to qualify the sticky black leather rolled front seat as a tattoo parlor.

Me and Shorty had been raisin hell in the southern county all night. It was now 1:00 a.m. and time to live up to all our evening's whispered and shouted expectations. Promises over the beer soaked blasts of the West Texas steel slide guitar music, double shot glasses clicking too many times per hour, occasional shrill squeaks from package- painted, bourbon sipping cowgirls of all intentions, each skunk doused with one of a million stifling perfumes.

Me and Shorty had a full night of bar hopping, the cowboys, truck drivers and poke up bra mamas as thick as the music and smoke with a certain sense of reckless excitement mingled with instant danger, when the tiger's back hairs bristle and stand at attention. A danger ever close when you have a cowboy bar, dance floor, cash paycheck Friday night, double shots and beer chasers as in Jack Daniels and a Bud.

As the wick of the evening fiercely burns on, tempers flare and, if not careful, you can take your front teeth home in a bag as in drunkenly staggering across the dusty dirt packed parking lot, winding through a sea of rust-stricken pick up trucks, occasionally stepping over a small puddle of foamy blood spittle or transmission fluid.

Parking lot exiting etiquette was strictly followed as we out-of-control fish tailed the Mustang through the lot with serious rubber meeting the road on the still warm asphalt, sweet southern night alcoholic death way, thirty-seven miles south of the Tennessee border.

Mary Sue Beth Ann, one of the five Skaggs sisters, now fourteen, pretty with a too mature body noticed by all. You could say she was one of those born to please young ladies. She was hot and I wanted her.

Bertram LeRoy Skaggs, Mary Sue Beth Ann's father was considered the hardest, meanest, son of a bitch in the mines, a tobacco spittin, dirty, two hundred forty pounder, without teeth and sienna tobacco stains from mouth corners to chin forming a peculiar facial downward arrowhead. When he clumsily spoke I was lightly atomized with a nasty batch of stale bourbon breath, tobacco juice, seasoned with frequently reshuffled slang, such as, "Shit-Fuck-Hell", "Hot Ole Mighty Damn" and "Dirty Bastard Bitch Fucker".

Daringly, I nervously told Bertam LeRoy that I was now fifteen and interested in his daughter Mary Sue Beth Ann and that we was old enough to be thinkin of a family and stuff and I might go to truck drivin school in Memphis, learn about big rigs and stuff and make beaucoup money, maybe even move away with Mary Sue Beth Ann.

Bertram LeRoy responded with the speed of a Venus Fly Trap cluching my throat; he clearly made his point, "Come round my spread and I'll kill you, boy, don't mess with me!"

Once Shorty needle tattooed my left arm with her name, I'd show it to her an her family anthey'd know that we wuz right for each other. Shorty first outlined her name on my arm with a ball point pen from the Devonsville, Tennessee, Dairy Tastee Freeze. There it was: Mary Sue Beth Ann in block letters. Shorty added a rose between the new red ink addition and the existing, slightly faded blue ink Lisa Ray Jean tattoo just above.

Shorty refilled the vets horse syringe in the wet, red ink sponge for an hour and a half completing his work. Burning, blood droplet patterned, I rubbed the proud new tattoo with a crumpled gas station paper towel soaked in Jim Beam as me an Shorty split the last of the bourbon, goosing the Mustang during each early morning sharp mountain curve, goin home laughin.

THE DO-DON'T MAN

Maybe it will and maybe it won't, maybe it do and maybe it don't, only the Do-Don't Man really knows. The Do-Don't Man continually murmured this phrase under his breath like a mantra ricocheting from a canyon wall.

During the late 1920s and early 30s, northern Kansas agonized over a slow but sure change in weather patterns. With sun-leathered skin, the bleached-denim tractor-riding wheat farmers grimaced while earth polished, bright steel tractor blades revealed increasing dust pockets in the hot blowing, freshly-loafed soil.

As aged molar teeth lightly ground on the land's increasingly inescapable dry grit, each farmer silently prayed for long overdue rain.

Rain, maybe it will, maybe it won't, maybe it do, maybe it don't. Only the Do-Don't Man knows.

Modest batten and board ranch houses perched miles apart on this tabletop terrain were typically surrounded by unending amber flowing seas of harvestable wheat. Not this time, no crop this year. The dwarfed wheat stocks were wind twisted and matted with the damnable choking dust.

Four poorly dressed kids to feed, a cigar box full of overdue maintenance equipment bills and that damn Union Bank president that always fiddles with his vested railroad watch every time he mentions foreclosure.

There is enough meat and provisions in the freezer box for two weeks or so. Damn! Our lives are increasingly desperate, even the children carry fear in their eyes as they shuffle their meager plate of beans, salt port and corn bread.

What next? Well, maybe it will and maybe it won't and maybe it do and maybe it don't. Only the Do-Don't Man knows.

Shared concerns and stories of long term failing crops were solemnly repeated by the farmers at the whitewashed, Silo County Grange Hall, No. 6. Farmers nervously tooth-picked their tobacco stained teeth and tinkered with the creases in their sweat-stained straw hats: yet there was no plan, no solution, no agrarian safety net for their dilemma. Even Elias, the silo grain operator, serving as our Sunday preacher, could offer only prayers and assistance with filing incomprehensible, bureaucratic forms for government subsidized bulk cheese and limited staples. What to do? Well, maybe it will and maybe it won't, and maybe it do and maybe it don't. Only the Do-Don't Man knows.

The small grange hall fell silent, and only the light hiss of the kerosene lanterns could be heard until, finally, Old Jack, a retired farmer injured years ago by a tractor overturn, screeched the legs of his chair upright as he slowly rose. With tattered hat and Bull Durham bag in hand, he addressed the cowboy-shirted farm hands, "I heard a rumor several days ago in Barrow County about a man walking through Kansas with the power to change fate. It may be bull crap, but this guy brought rain recently to three northern counties, and he is supposed to be slowly coming this way."

The majority of the reality calloused farmers dismissed such an idea as absurd. How could some story book magic man change the weather? Well, maybe he can and maybe he can't, and maybe he do and maybe he don't. Only the Do-Don't Man really knows.

Little Sara, the Jacobsen's middle daughter, was the first to spot him deliberately shuffling toward the six grain silos, general store and single pump gas station that comprised the city, Evansville, population 116, Silo County, Kansas.

She was totally out of breath as she side stepped the broken porch planking, opening the torn and squeaky kitchen screen door, "He's coming, I just saw him walking from the north east towards the silos. It's him, Mom, it's that guy Dad mentioned that can make stuff right, that maybe it do and maybe it don't man." Her mother's eyes widened as she ground corn meal and stoked the smoldering, blackened pot belly stove. "He's a stranger, stay away from him like I told you, go get your brother and tell your dad there is a man up on the road and take this Mason jar of sugared beans for his lunch without spilling them." Could this be the Do-Don't Man? Well, maybe it is and maybe it ain't, and maybe he do and maybe he don't.

Irma Gale Lee, the local crank-generated telephone operator and the community's ongoing gossip champion, spread the news with the speed of a wind-whipped prairie fire, resulting in a rare mid day impromptu grange hall meeting.

Bug-splattered and rusted older Ford pick up trucks and tractors surrounded the grange hall. Farmers and families gathered beneath the hall's roof overhang, the only available retreat from the blistering Kansas sun. The sometimes Sunday preacher brought the attentive group to order by tapping his pipe on the grange pump handle. "We need someone to meet with this Do-Don't Man; old Jack is the oldest, been here the longest and can speak our mind." The families nodded with approval, and Jack set out for the silos. Would this work, could he help us? Maybe he can and maybe he can't and maybe he will and maybe he won't, only the Do-Don't Man knows.

As Jack and the closely following families approached the silos, there stood the Do-Don't Man on the heat compacted road. Tall, dead silent, and clad in black from head to foot, his straight brimmed felt hat topped the oiled, cracked light canvas cape, suitable gear for any weather.

The two moved in slow circles around one another like curious sniffing dogs searching for some unobtainable clue. Facing one another, old Jack told the story of dust blown crops and bare knuckle hard times. The Do-Don't Man locked his gaze on Jack as he plead for help. "Help. Maybe I can and maybe I can't, and maybe I will and maybe I won't, and maybe I do and maybe I don't."

Thoughtfully parting, the Do-Don't Man asked the people to meet at the edge of the town with him at sunrise with all their worldly possessions. Changing one's fate always has an associated price.

Each family member laid their most important possession on the knife-scarred kitchen table: a thumb worn prairie Bible, a genuine English porcelain doll with a carved wood substitute left arm, a railroad watch and chain, two pink pressed glass bowls from Germany, several antique silver dollars, hand decorated silver candelabra, numerous rings, silver spurs, and an eight day clock with a curved glass face. These worldly possessions linked the farmers to happier times and memories, their last grasp on their earlier lives.

The families moved by lantern and solemnly assembled at the edge of town before sunrise. Soon the Do-Don't Man would come, and their futures would be traded for all their worldly possessions assembled in an orderly fashion on the handmade quilt at the roadside. Would it work, was this the right thing to do? Well, maybe it is and maybe it ain't, and maybe it do and maybe it don't, only the Do-Don't Man really knows.

As the sun rays evaporated the wheat-stalk webs of dew, the Do-Don't Man slowly approached the assembled crescent of families. Boldly and deliberately he delivered his message, "I have the power to do, I have the power to don't, the power to will, and the power to won't. Now repeat after me," he beckoned. At first in a low voice, then louder, the farmers chanted with the Do-Don't Man arms above their heads swaying left to right with each verse. Maybe it will, maybe it won't, maybe it do maybe it don't, only the Do-Don't Man knows. As the chanting crescendoed, the Do-Don't Man crisply snapped his long fingers, commanding silence.

"The power to do and the power to don't lies within each of these two stones," he noted carefully pulling a small polished black lacquered wood case from beneath his cape. Freeing the brass latch, he revealed the burgundy velvet interior where two separate stones nested, each the same size, shape, color and texture. "Each of these stones provides separate results when rubbed," he explained.

Turning his back to the families, he extended cape-draped arms above his head, forming a bat-like tent while he barely whispered, "Maybe I will and maybe I won't, maybe I do and maybe I don't." The Do-Don't Man slowly lowered his arms and, turning to the group, tipped his hat while he placed the carefully folded quilt of worldly possessions under his cape and slowly continued his journey through Kansas. Did it work, will it save us? Well, maybe it will and maybe it won't, and maybe it do and maybe it don't. Only the Do-Don't Man knows.

As an unexpected veil of cloud momentarily blocked the stinging rays of the sun, the first drops were felt. Doubting and uncertain, a few sporadic drops of fickle rain produced small, rising, donut-shaped dust clouds where silver dollar size drops began pelting the thickly-layered road dust like bullets. With abandonment and disbelief, the eye widening Kansans began to shriek and hug in the increasing downpour. Children forgivingly heel-stomped, quickly forming mud puddles speckling everyone with the begged-for muddy water.

The chameleon sky rapidly transformed to heavy pillowed rain clouds as far as the eye could see. The distinctive odor of ozone molecules filled the nostrils as nearby thunderbolts cracked and the rains increased. Wet and exasperated, the jubilant band ran toward town for cover.

The base of empty grain silo no. 4 provided the closest available shelter, a towering space clad in corrugate galvanized sheet metal with huge rotary vents at the silo peak.

The mud-splattered, rain-soaked families ran inside the silo panting, wiping rain and perspiration from their matted foreheads. Abruptly stopping, everyone fell silent. There, dead center, on the middle of the silo floor, lay the quilt, flat and without a crease, with all of their worldly possessions neatly assembled. In the center of the quilt sat the open velvet-lined black lacquered box containing only one stone, a stone that, when rubbed, changed fate.

Well, is that the do or the don't stone? Maybe it is and maybe it ain't, and maybe it do and maybe it don't. Only the Do-Don't Man <u>really</u> knows.

DOG HOUSE

As man's best friend, I respectfully request that my quality of life be mankind improved for myself and serve as a model for the benefit of all caninehood.

We understand each other: the pats, sniffs, scratches, tongue licks, tail wags and those glassy, long, unbroken, brown-eyed looks that say so much.

I've been dog dreamin" a lot lately: renovation, addition, maybe an entirely new designer dog house and, as my loving master, hope you will consider the following doggie design issues.

Cold, garden hose spray baths, using the old sponge in the garage with laundry detergent makes my skin itch and the beach towel drying leaves me smelling like sun screen, the current joke of all neighborhood females.

Canine sexual privacy: well, would you prefer backyard cheering neighbors watching open arena doggie style games with your lover or the intimate trappings of a backroom canine pleasure den? For the record, we enjoy a variety of sexual positions other than the overly advertized doggie style requiring privacy and several special love toys.

We prefer private toilet facilities: this shivering in the rain while display squatting has no class. Additionally, tracking us with clear plastic bags and close up encounters with designer catalog poop shovels while relieving ourselves is plain insensitive.

Millie, a female collie on my mother's side, growls that we deserve fresh, balanced meals, attractively served. May I suggest a typical meal be delivered in a three compartment silver steam plate containing a medium rare six to eight ounce t-bone, bone in please, vegetables, if floated in people gravy, and chocolate pudding. Napkins are not preferred.

Dog days occur three or four times a year: they are like PMS, better to just not ask questions and bond with us the following day.

My ideal doggie digs deserve to be equal to your love for me, I therefore propose the following. A newly architecturally designed environment of western red cedar enclosure - ticks hate cedar - a private cuddle room, a nose operated chilled water cooler, night light, trap door for wayward cats, tiered storage for various aged bones, overnight canine guest accommodations, a polished brass door entry graphic titled "World's Greatest Dog", a "Back In 10 Minutes" sign and framed interior photos of Pluto, Rin Tin Tin, and Lassie.

I would love rubbing my back on oil teak flooring beneath tinted glass skylights. Additionally, a thick fleeced nap pad and piped music would be a nice touch, music selections should not include "Oh Where, Oh Where Has My Little Doge Gone?" or "You Ain't Nothing But a Hound Dog".

Grant me all this and you may share my new house any night you experience marital differences.

GATOR JUSTICE

Mr. Edgar C. and Alley D. Gator, four legged, Southern Florida, heat baked alligators, healthy, always hungry, curious and subject to occasional, unannounced mood swings when provoked. From fumbling hatchlings barely able to swim, to fully developed four hundred pound hide covered muscle, complete with a very business like set of algae stained teeth, Edgar and Ally were always together.

True swamp mates, mentors of the local gator clan, grand gator wizard status at the elite members only Tale and Claw Club and famous for their renegade late night on land excursions.

The younger, two footer male gators hissed and growled praise as Edgar and Ally effortlessly tail powered by, the murky water wake revealing their hero's names on their wet gator tank tops. Last year Edgar received the Okeefanoke distinguished gator award and the most eligible bachelor over four hundred pound class belonged to Ally.

They gracefully navigated the western drainage ditch at midnight, up past the flake rusted irrigation pump controls and drippingly raised their leather pursed bellies onto the edge of the rear 7/11 oil stained parking lot. They winked the all clear sign, like gators often do, and clawed their way to the overfilled dumpster, one of their favorite stops. Edgar then did one of his best tricks, actually took several steps to the dumpster on his hind legs. While kangaroo like tail balancing, he snout thrusted the debris, flipping cans, and half eaten dumb people food to the lot for Ally's further inspection. Not a good score, same old regular people trash, not even a candy wrapper or stale sugar donut. Edgar, however, did keep the 1997 Buick owner's manual gripped in his jaw and snarled that he liked the pictures and loved the smell of the taco sauce stained binder.

After surgically chomping through the store's outside wall mounted telephone line and quickly swallowing the curious looking yellow pages, they slithered back into the swamp's broken reeded-canal and surface cruised toward home with the car manual and a stray newspaper stuck on Ally's hind claw.

Steaming in the veiled foggy morning swamp island sun, Edgar slowly claw turned the pages of the Buick manual, hissing at the people pictured on the pages of the owner's instruction book. Hell, he mused, he could operate one of these, but he would probably need to chomp out a large hole in the driver's seat to accommodate his tail.

Ally spread the smeared newsprint on the oozing mud bank and bellowed in disbelief at what he read. A local developer, Mr. Peter Profit, was advertising future residential view lots at Blue Marsh Lagoon, sited in the exact midst of their natural habitat, noting the swamp would be drained to accommodate roads and utilities.

Edgar and Ally snarled with rage at this threatening idea, twitching their nubby hided tails and gnashing their never flossed algae stained teeth in disgust, vowing to intervene. The ad listed Peter Profit's address, a posh location, but 16 miles away, a rolling development at Red Palmetto Acres.

Late Saturday evening, Edgar and Ally toured the drainage ditch, four glowing eyes cruising the ivory moonlit ripples to the nearly deserted 7/11 greedy people spot. Ally's eyes widened, could it be, really, a maroon 1997 Buick, windows down and rabbit footed key chain dangling from the ignition. Dare they, Ally approached cautiously, controlling his scratching claws on the oil spotted asphalt. Edgar, more determined than curious, snout dripping on the leatherette front seat, smiled that slow alligator smile, content that the dash board arrangement matched what he memorized in the Buick owner's manual.

After the secret alligator wink, tufted upholstery quickly flew as tail holes were crudely chomped. Springs and seat backs gave way to their surgical row of jagged teeth.

Edgar, now behind the chrome ringed steering wheel, clawed at the ignition while Ally fiddled with the shifter. With a burning lurch of screeching tires, they s-curved from the lot onto Route 17, the road to Peter Profit's Red Palmetto Acres.

Driving was more than a challenge, with more than one on-coming car veering off the road; after all, claw driving isn't easy, especially when you're lower right claw covers both the gas and brake pedals.

There, the loop on the left; that's it: 1384 Lagoon Loop, the Profit residence. Edgar veered onto the moonlit curved driveway, manicuring the low plantings with the fishtailing Buick, lurching to a skidding stop directly in front of the four car garage. Edgar's scarred right claw poked at the ignition but hit the radio. Ear splitting Rock music careened off the covered entry and lights came on as the double teak entry doors parted, revealing an obviously upset pokadot pajama clad Peter Profit.

He raced to the car but abruptly jolted back as Edgar's saliva drooled over the car door chrome. Meanwhile, FiFi, his pom pom tailed, Las Vegas rhinestone collared poodle erratically circled the car, nervously pee squatting wet poodle puddles ever few feet. Ally snatched Fifi gingerly by the collar and quickly stashed the whimpering dog in the trunk, unharmed.

"Stop the development immediately and we won't have a poodle dinner. Cooperate and your frufru yapper will be delivered unharmed at the 7/11 site Friday night. One more thing, no police or animal control officers or she's a goner."

Thursday, Ally squinted at the news rack, "Developer stops residential project." Victory at last.

Fifi quivered on Ally's back like a nervous sea captain as he slow tailed to the 7/11 lot Friday night. She bounded to Peter Profit's Mercedes coupe unharmed.

Edgar and Ally chuckled as they submerged back into the canal; environmental justice was served and the Buick driving would make a grand dinner time story tonight.

WORLD TRUTH

Ya know, there's just a lotta stuff in life that you accept as truth; you haven't tested it but take it as fact. History, geography, physics, we sponge absorb all of it, even though we never set foot in Madagascar or verify the viscosity of inclined planes, we simply swallow all of it as true. True until the acceptance foundation shakes and crumbles.

Rock climbing through the High Sierras, I bug-like picked my way up a partially collapsed gorge of sharp edged gray peppered granite. Dwarfed timberline fir and that pine needle perfumed rock baked air, even the ever persistent sweat flies were on their afternoon break. As I turtle-walked to the top, I was met with a total wash of high altitude crystal blue mountain sky and a level band of palomino colored heat punished sand. A strip at the edge of a continuous stone cliff set ten feet back from the unexpected cliff face, a steel woven wire mesh fence, 12 feet high with posted signs, bearing a government message "Official End of The Earth, area beyond cliff face is considered out of this world. For information contact sentry at closest guard tower." What the hell, we trusted them and they never told us about the end of the earth border or described the location of out of this world; I can only suppose that it's some well kept military secret.

Gilbert Blaylock manned guard tower No. 6 for 11 years and would rattle off his general orders while ogling over a cluster of green glowing computer screens, each framing the absolute nothingness of the eight nighttime high resolution security cameras. Popping spent pumpkin seed shells as thick rubber soles shuffled about the tower, Gilbert explained the end of the earth border. All the great and small world ideas were hurled by several large catapults projected into the air with great force and speed, all boxed and crated for air travel, and all targeted to fall within the established limits of our known civilized world. This is where the end of this world becomes critical: all hurled objects landing over the fence could not be claimed and considered as ideas simply out of this world.

Gilbert patiently answered all my questions and even agreed to escort me through an electrified gate to the sharp cliff face. There, far below, an endless sea of crates and boxes: some old, some fresh, most partially cracked and splintered. All of the out of this world ideas had just barely missed the top barb wire strands of this world's fence and now were gone forever, even the several snared at the top had fallen to the other side. Gilbert knew where they all were down there, when they landed, and each of their contents. Most were graphically titled and dated: 1953, cure for cancer; 1974, food source powder to end world hunger; 1982, absolute cure for all romantic heartbreaks; and the 1993 pills to stop all snoring and farting.

The below textured carpet of contraptions, inventions and ideas pin-dotted the landscape as far as I could see, a pocked graveyard of brilliance, dedication and heartbreak. Checking his records, Gilbert pointed far off to a small heap of broken boxes and using his magnified spotting scope, I saw my name neatly stenciled on several crates. The one to the left was that sparky brunette with the overly developed breasts. Now that crate I can understand because she really was out of this world, and the ones beside it such as my 5th grade plan to parachute off the roof with a bed sheet or to put acid in the public water supply, those ideas were probably better over the top strand.

As Gilbert and I chatted, the two police blue lights of his monitor counsel staccato flashed to a synchronized 80 decibel buzzer; the lights lowered in the dark, blue-green electronic counsel. Gilbert snapped into his too-well worn alert mode, quickly flipping chrome toggle switches and thumb rolling calibrated dials. He abruptly announced "incoming" in an almost barking Pekinese voice. There to the left, see the red streak in the sky, it's gonna be real close, whoa! Just cleared the top wire to out of this world, the electronic print out indicates this as a Congressional budget approval package and there goes another crate, over the top, not even close.

Gilbert told me that I must leave during the night so as not to be seen; the half moon would permit barely enough light to descend the gorge. After sunset Gilbert said he must follow careful procedures: photographing, fingerprinting, weighing and blood typing me. I signed and thumb printed an agreement to secrecy and was told a government official would visit me within four days.

Under the silver blue mountain moon, I descended the silent ageless stone brittle peaks, pausing to inhale the total solitude. Then a low, red cinder crate rocketed just a hundred feet or so above me, powdering its path with sparks and a vacuum of hot wind. Headed for the fence alright and maybe high enough to stay in this world. Then, a second package rotating as it streaked over the gorge top. A quick fleeting glimpse of the marked contents as they hurtled by read: "spiritual enlightenment".

EUROPE IN STYLE

The worn, smooth, oak night stick of the German policeman beat an uncomfortable rhythm on my vulnerable exposed knees, probably the beat of some earlier Reichstag military troop marching song. Firm and painful, the blows jerked me from my unsettled sleep to a state of adrenaline focused reality.

The instant life decision choice flashed before me, "Should I try and deck this guy or run?"

Leaning over me was a gorilla bodied, sausage breathed, very intense, gray clad Deutsche policeman, spitting German commands at point blank range. I spoke no German.

As I was Teutonically escorted to the Hamburg train station exit, a passing Frenchman murmured, "You can't sleep in the train station!"

My black booted policeman pointed through the etched glass station exit doors into the cold, rainy, downtown street-reflecting Hamburg night. A tuck under my arm small travel bag with toothbrush, soap, map, one shirt and passport. Not the best scene to be broke, wet and hungry into the night with the "time to live by your wits" button on.

Too early to forage on easy prey hard rolls snagged in hanging mesh bags on residential door knobs and too wet outside, I targeted any dry, warm opportunity.

A smallish pension with a second floor lobby, just maybe; the door release buzzed as I entered a small foyer. From the above lobby a voice gruffly belted a question and I froze in silence, then, nothing. At least I was dry and off the streets.

After several minutes of strained listening, I crept to the carpeted mid stair landing, cat curled, half sleeping in half dry clothing.

Hearing the slow heel cobble of the concierge unexpectedly descending the upper stair tier, I knee jerk bolted down to the lobby street level.

Desperate, I unlatched the triangular below stair storage door joining mops and bottles of sleeping German cleansers and disinfectants. Pulling the heavy door behind me, the latching hardware seated firmly with a heavy weight metallic ring.

Total blackout, no air, slightly panicked, quickly moving, hopeful braille hands longed for the soothing touch of an internal door latch or light switch. Nine, nada, none to be found! I was trapped in the wedge shaped, under stair tomb of King Bill the Dumb with soapy embalming fluids complete with toilet paper roll mummy wrappings.

The stifling dead air cloaked me in a veil of beaded perspiration and uncomfortable itching. I shed my shirt in this black hole steam bath, later followed by trousers and shorts. Like an entree served on a bed of shredded lettuce, I finally fell into an uneasy sleep on a thick layer of finely shredded packing paper.

The deadbolt snapped and the door arched fully open, bright blinding sun revealed an alarmed, back sprawled nude partially feathered in small strips of clinging colored packing paper.

Clearly in shock, the stout, elderly cleaning lady dropped her broom and took three sharp inhalations before her first shriek for policia while I Indian danced on one leg trying to mount my jeans, like a bobbing, paper feathered bird jumping to the beat of the cleaning lady's now operatic shrieks.

Half awake, half dressed, half papered and half running, I hit the street promising to visit next time with a little more money and a little more class.

LIVIN' BY WITS

Funny how some stuff in life takes on a different importance: like the value of a toothbrush when you don't have one or clean socks when you own only one pair.

My first paycheck at the hellish brass foundry winged me to the downtown Army Surplus store; you know, the kind that sells everything from gas masks to camouflage tents, all displayed on painted mannequins with chipped thumbs and noses. I filled an over sized paper bag with shorts, socks, denim shirt, kakhis and essential toiletries, just enough to fill the drapery cord clothes line with sink washed clothing in my borderline hotel warren. I also scored a single electric hot plate, can opener, canned ravioli and crackers and boosted a fork and spoon from the metal tabled work cafeteria.

I had landed. Shaved, showered, dressed in cheap casual clothes, a hot plate dinner of canned ravioli behind me, twenty-six dollars in cash and takin' it all to the simmering LA streets at 8:30 Saturday night.

Carless, the downtown corridor became my evening playpen, an urban turf stippled with international immigrants and small storefront marginal businesses, that except for the Pakistani family operated liquor stores, clammed shut at sunset with creaking accordion grills or steel roll down doors.

Nearer the square, a handful of bars served finger marked glasses of cheap Muscatel and shell glasses of flat draft beer. Each single barman knew his bobbing string of derelict customers by name and alcoholic capacity. Two hands trembling to lift the wine glass, the bristle bearded crowd with the matted gray hair peered from deep set, red rimmed eyes, momentarily calculating the presence of a stranger, then returning to their jabber, arguing the essence of nothing with their scab cheeked partner.

A shot of bourbon and a small beer chaser downed as I nodded in agreement and slid two Camel cigarettes to the babbling, strongly scented, alcoholic pilot fish now by my side. Saluting, I heel clicked over the worn linoleum patterned floor to the sparkling concrete sidewalk that borders Pershing Square, a concentrated test tube of sin - just five blocks away.

By 9:30 p.m. the perimeter of the palm studded square thumped with activity, mostly of the kind not discussed in detail during church socials. The unspoken caste system was well tonight and fully in place. Over perfumed strolling young female hookers in their satin hot pants along the north east side. Skin tight bleached leather boys, one knee bent are propping the retail store fronts along the south and west. All being busily circled by an array of flesh pleasure seekers, men, women, young, old, gay and straight, all playing their fantasy cash-for-sex card.

Street workers quickly develop an important working sense of sorting all sidewalk workers and Johns, and can spot the license prefix and small wave radio trunk aerial on any darkblue or tan, four door Ford Crown Victoria vice car from 500 yards. As the slow cruising, gum chewing vice cops fish eye the Square for regulars and Johns, all goes limp. Hookers spin to look in storefronts, their most pasted-on Christian faces reflected in the untruthful glass. "Just shoppin for my mama," the teenage Puerto Rican calls to the passing police as she blows a kiss while slightly shaking her money maker.

The photo-sweet, steroid munching, leather boys quickly form groups of three or four and feint loud arguments of baseball scores and the championship Lakers.

All know the calloused game too well including all the carnival barker dressed pimps. One of man's contemporary rituals unfolding right in front of you. Buzzing the pulsing skin hive and trading LA night secret desires for carefully folded sheaves of Jacksons and Franklins.

I took my position mid-block off the southeast corner of the Square, an unspoken location for a variety of cruising females seeking short term male companionship. In the lineup along the wall with three other young guys, I first noticed Elaine, a fairly good looking middle aged prospect, comfortable in her two year old Mercedes coupe. She made three slow passes around the Square, each time pausing at curbside to eyeball the meat rack. The fourth round she stopped directly in front of me. As the passenger window powered down, she pointed at me, then curled her index finger, and unlatching the door, she patted the rolled leather seat. I slid into comfort and the game began.

A classy, middle aged tennis player with an interest in Japanese art and ritual, always with those lucky, light green jade rings dangling from her neck. Elaine and I rendezvoused for two months, small talking of Japanese architecture while frequenting several of the shops and restaurants in LA's Japan Town. Elaine offered exciting moments, was generous without embarrassment, tipped well and was pleasant company, sort of my supplementary ticket to some LA fun.

Our relationship ended on an off note, perhaps just getting too accustomed to one another, but like stale crackers, you eat em if you're hungry enough.

We heard Ella at the Hollywood Bowl, real knock out stuff and zig zagged to dinner in Japan Town, a special, upper end restaurant with tiered cushioned seating and bamboo reed sandals for everyone. Floating candles in lotus glass bowls, Geisha servers and the light background whining of the Japanese violin, great ambiance even for a legitimate couple.

Buoyed by the concert, Elaine ordered two Black Russians, heavy on the vodka and light on Japanese custom. We dined on the upper tier, overlooking the curved, coliseum-seated diners below us. Tasty delicate courses, doused with an over supply of Black Russians. During the last course the vodka blacksmith hammered me. By now the room was tilting and the vodka and butterflied shrimp were scurrying toward my stomach's exit sign. Cross legged I rose from my pillow, instantly losing my balance, dragging a tangled reed mat with my right foot and dead reckoned for the mens room. First kneeling, then completely falling into the lower seating tier, I nested on my side, soaked in sour soup atop a middle aged couple. Clawing away teapots, candles and noodle splattered drinks, I bounced to the main exit through a quickly widening group of short, drop jawed, wide eyed Japanese business men.

Never turning back, I reeled all the way to my little hotel by foot, partially digested shrimp and curly crispy noodles now decorating my lower trouser legs and those silly bamboo sandals.

Not my best night: I never saw Elaine or my black, size 10 loafers again, but in sunny California the sun would surely shine on Pershing Square again tomorrow.

DINNER WITH JESUS

God! These jeans, knee worn and washer dryer wise, never thought I would actually die in these. The sun faded Nascar tee shirt and ever ready deck shoes complete my death duds wardrobe.

Dad would have preferred a crisper haircut; Mom, creased trousers and shined shoes, but the chill of death slipped silently into my room without warning and offered a final invitation to come as you are.

A scant handful of us newly deads fell into a precarious category as borderline heaven or hell candidates, requiring a finalizing face to face dinner interview with Jesus.

Some luck, I thought, as I was escorted to the private dining area and seated at a table for two. The short winged maitre de angel told me Jesus was peace making in Africa and would be a few minutes behind schedule. I nervously shuffled the flatware, while pretending to study the menu.

Flanked by two cherubic angels, he floated to his seat, a real aura around his head as he ordered bread and wine. Feinting my disdain for alcohol, I ordered sparkling water and the special - fishes and loaves.

Mid meal he asked if I had seen my final good-evil spreadsheet. Slipping the heavenly palm pilot from his white linen tunic, his brow slightly furrowed as he tapped in my entry.

"Hmmm, really a tough call, Bill."

I plastered on my most innocent face and we ate in silence.

Eventually he gazed at me saying things did not look particularly promising. As a final desperate measure I insisted on paying the bill, he conceded and covered the tip with a worn gold Roman coin, a bust of Julius Caesar still barely visible.

As a last ditch effort, I almost jokingly asked if he was a betting man, a simple Roman coin toss, heads heaven, tails hell, what do you say, JC?

The attending angels blushed as he aptly flipped the coin, mid air I called heads, it landed on his nail scarred wrist, Caesar side up, heads, I won!

He warmly congratulated me, quickly winking while excusing himself for a near by conference with the Pope regarding available Catholic tax shelters.

Angels immediately flooded the dining room, effortlessly carrying me to Heaven's Gate,. bearing chilled quality champagne and Thai sticks. I willingly agreed to be bathed. Yep, this was Heaven alright.

The new tuxedo and shoes were perfect as I slipped into the leather tufted, velvet trimmed Heavenly love seat. While reclined I felt a light tingling mound at each of my shoulder blades rising, I removed my jacket and cumberbund, then the shirt.

I was pleasantly startled to see two budding Angel wings. Damn, I really did make it!

NURSE DORTEA

The salty, round, black machined like rocks rolled with the cradle of each wave, wet and clicking like thousands of castanets. Early, French Riviera sunrise reflected a pinkish cadre of Cote Azure beach stones, each with their own private Rivera story, locked and sworn to stone, silence forever.

I uncomfortably spent last night with damp sand as my bed. Ironically, across the ocean highway from the Grande Hotel stood the epitome accommodations of international grand pomp and excessiveness. Mysterious dark windowed Bentley sedans and guest introductions at the champagne flower gardens. Small armies of French speaking Pakistani hotel staff in board stiff starched white jackets chirping "Welcome to the Grande Hotel, how may I help you?" Well, not this time, maybe the corner suite in my next lifetime.

Hungry and damp I prodded to the highway while my things to do today targeted food, hot shower and a ride to Paris. Student ship from Rotterdam to New York in eight days.

The Goddess of hitchhiking was merciful as a Parisian plated sedan slowed along side, a strikingly attractive smiling female driver offered a ride. Dortea was quite a package by any standards.

Our language barrier quickly gave way to hand motions, backyard Spanish, map pointing and laughter. A score! I was Paris bound.

Late morning we added a third: a stocky, Aryan, German student that willingly became our translator with his perfected French and English, rollicking over mistranslated jokes and travel tales.

Pulling up to a Bistro for lunch, I feinted an upset stomach and insisted on remaining perched in the car. As they dined, I began to wonder if the tufted leather seat upholstery might be edible.

They returned with butcher paper wrapped bread and cheese and my hunger was quickly revealed.

Our small international trio threaded onward toward the City of Light, vacuumed toward the kinetic mysteries and corners of Paris.

Thanks to the ever present generosity of Dortea, Hans and I were treated to a delightful early dinner; we thoroughly enjoyed each other's company and during dinner Dortea and I locked eyes for a second or so too long, secretly signaling a growing magnetism.

After an hour or so we bid Aufweidersein to our German companion, leaving him on the southern rim of urban hard Paris.

I brokenly asked if she would drop me at the least expensive hotel room, while sheepishly brandishing my bag of small, multi countried denomination coins, coins too petty to change at currency exchanges yet my entire traveling fortune valued at perhaps three dollars American.

She politely inspected two hotels that will never be listed in tour book accommodations. Noticeably saddened she abruptly announced that I could share her inner city flat until morning. I was gratified as we collected bread, wine, cheeses and coffee to be shared at her high ceilinged eclectically furnished flat. She enjoyed good natural light and a postcard view of the city that shimmers in light rain like all the Post Impressionist paintings found in expensive, rarely opened, upper New York coffee table books.

I was offered fresh towels and a bath at the end of the hall. Refreshingly returning to her flat, I entered into a different world of colorful veiled light fixtures, sandalwood incense, clusters of burning candles and a transformed Dortea with out stretched arms, sculpturally clad in a black transparent veil. My damp towel, clothing and her veil quickly found their new home on the floor by her beautifully curved, upwardly arching feet.

We spun into a clutching passionate dance of ecstacy. Her shimmering, candlelit white body gracefully butterflied around and through me. She was the Olympic princess of prolonging multiple sensual pleasures. We were hungry for one another, sexually feasted and fell asleep laughing in our irreversible web of arms and legs. I felt her heart beat against my ribcage as we drifted into a totally satisfying love sleep.

The next morning found me silently rehearsing my sweetest hospitality lines. Her arms folded softly around me producing a hot cup of strong French coffee with her suggestion that I stay a few days, tour Paris alone by day and love-dine our early evenings together. I was flattered, loved the opportunity and toured museums, gardens and cafes by day and relished pleasure by night. She generously left a neatly folded stack of Francs on the carved walnut dresser corner each morning for my daytime adventures. Gazing from the third floor flat window, Paris swarmed below, hunched elderly women peeking behind scarves, white trousered meat and bread delivery men, uniformed school children, damp street cobblestones with granite curbs and the thin veil of spent diesel fuel. I held the winning lottery ticket for seven days and nights of French heaven.

We both sensed our coming parting, doubly sweetening our last evening together, two people locked in French-Anglo tenderness. The morning of the eighth day we nibbled baguettes and jabbered like chimps as she steadily pointed the maroon Renault sedan toward the Belgian border. Our conversation diminished as the border unstoppably neared. In light rain we traded our last kisses and tears, you know, the kind of tears that drip hot on your cheek.

I stepped into the drizzle leaving a rose bouquet on the leather seat as she slowly pulled away toward Paris. I unblinkingly gazed until sweet Dortea evaporated into the gray horizon.

The day after graduating from architecture school I boarded a student ship in New York bound to Rotterdam to pursue graduate studies in Stockholm. Of course the first stop would be Paris and Dortea. I motorcycled straight to Paris and arrived at Dortea's flat feeling my pulse quicken with anticipation. I longed to mold her in my arms and caress her scented neck. I anxiously rang the matronly building custodian and an elderly, gray bunned, Gitine smoking, apron clad woman appeared jabbering in French. She stubbed her smoldering cigarette out in the concrete sidewalk joint as I repeated "Dortea, Dortea Thiebald, Apartment 3." She crimped her brows and rubbed the side of her bulbous nose, occasionally twisting several of her long chin hairs as she responded, "Ah, Dortea, Dortea Thiebald, live here but during the season is in Cannes and Nice, prostituta for Riviera season and nurse prosituta here in off season."

My lightly perspiring spine stiffened and I felt the cool dry rush of reality. The puzzle pieces quickly goose stepped into place. The sweet truth, Dortea was a woman of the night in her white shortened skirt and neck line plunging nursing uniform.

I was heartfully stunned yet could only admire her once in a lifetime generosity, hospitality and love.

I never saw Dortea again. I have silently and delicately folded her into the creased pages of a wonderful love history.

MONKEY BUSINESS

Yes, upper Briarwood, secluded, very exclusive, gated and secure, upper Connecticut money, deep in the valley of historic estates and trophy corporate residences, the home of Dr. Carl Bantu and his dreadful, medicated wife Eve. Carl and Eve, charity benefit trusts, opening opera and symphony party hosts, board members and chairmanships, all the social page trappings that attach like magnets to real wealth.

You might say Carl and Eve had it all: he, a well published and renowned American biologist, now retired, with several animals elegantly housed in a stone clad one estate library, a Romanesque jewel that now accommodated some of the doctors once experimental or poached specimens including, two middle-aged parrots, a Llama, two cougars, three spider monkeys and the pride of the collection, Olga, a very special five year old female chimpanzee.

Eve, a woman of eastern seaboard culture, boarding prep schools, appropriate social introductions, Vassar, Brown crowd, Harvard, Yale rowing matches and apparent receivership to her father's copper mine industrial fortune.

Now seemingly resigned to an unfulfilled life, Eve is heavy handed with the vodka and Carl seems to retreat further from a failing 41 year marriage.

Once, fiery in love, young then, he a young veterinarian, she a charity celebrity, the pool of love slowly but surely dried to a stain of sameness, as some loves can do and Eve and Carl desperately sought private roads on loves unmarked highways.

Eve's early afternoons and evenings focused on ongoing conversations with her scrapbook of social events, the Shorenstein's Bar Mitzvah, summer party fundraiser's, teas with the art commission - logarithmically staged with innocent looking iced vodka in crystal art glasses, moans and tears, and the tell-tale increased volume control with each Italian aria. The once socially dazzling Eve met the vodka monster and typically red lined by 8:30, leaving Carl to his own pursuits.

Carl met Olga at a native animal traders on the edge of the steamy dripping rain forest. From behind the freshly cut lashed bamboo cage, first eye contact between Carl and Olga, everything froze in time and Olga's shining dark brown, wet eyes knew that she and the curious looking biologist would pursue their limits.

Carl offered fresh fruit, clean water and a free ticket from the cruel wire snare traps of the forest poachers. Carl's experiments with Olga never materialized; yet he always managed to keep her about and sometimes during late evenings he would pull his over stuffed leather lounge chair to her cage and and speak to her between Cuban cigars and brandy.

When Carl spoke, Olga listened intently; when he finished, she would slowly roll her extended puckered lips, wrap her arms over her black bristle haired body and offer a low tone, taken by Carl as a gesture of compassionate and understanding sympathy.

Evenings repeated and Carl had his favorite den modified with the addition of Olga's cage, now near the fireplace and library, a much cozier arrangement for their shared late evenings.

When Carl was on errands, Eve would often show her disdain for Olga. Eve criticized the cage addition at the den, and frequently teased Olga by pulling shut the blackout drape on Olga's cage or moving her fruit tray out of reach. When their eyes met, Olga's teeth were bared and she shriek jumped with wildly flapping arms, hurling her metal water bowl as Eve fled.

It all started innocently and playfully enough. Olga, let from her cage and in the oak trimmed den after wifey was well off to sleep, Carl poured brandy, two inches in the cut crystal glasses, this time for both of them. The mood music seemed to sooth the chimp and after two bananas, two brandies and half a cigar, Carl smiled while offering Olga one of Eve's long abandoned silk teddies. Olga coquettishly moved to her cage to change as Carl further intensified the mood music.

Reappearing, Olga, a bit squat, very muscular and quite hairy in the now splitting silk teddy, showed surprising agility as she clutched Carl to dance; swaying slowly to the music, they formed an interesting couple: Carl, knees bent and stooping over in his tasseled smoking jacket; Olga standing on his slippers, hairy arms around his neck.

Who knows where all this could go. As the evening steamed on, Olga became more passionate, dropping an unpeeled banana onto Carl's crotch and retrieving it several times, then loudly smacking her lips and sucking Carl's neck and wrists. Shortly hereafter, during a moment of jungle passion, she tore the lower left arm from Carl's jacket.

As they danced during the early morning, Eve's face surprisingly appeared from behind the oak paneled den entry doors. Horrified at Carl in his boxer shorts, the blue ones with the butterflies, and Olga in her now shredded and banana stained teddy. Outraged, she grabbed Olga by one arm and moved toward the cage. As the stainless steel hinged door opened, Olga scampered around Eve and leapt on her back, forcing Eve into the cage. Quickly bolting the tamper proof slide lock, Carl padlocked the door, throwing the key randomly into a desk drawer.

Eve cried and plead within her new caged home. As Olga delivered Eve's evening meal of cold oatmeal, carefully eyeballing her for a full minute, Olga turned up the music, snapped shut the blackout curtain at Eve's cage and started that slow dancin' number so she and Carl could let that sweet monkey business begin.

NIGHT FRIGHT

Several times so far this lifetime, I vividly recall the rush of my hair standing up from fright, totally electrifying and almost out of body. The rush of air by the ears, the thunderbolt through the spine, that tinkling sensation when the world halts in suspension, the commanding moment when fright crashes uninvitedly through your ceiling. Those times in life when you unwillingly compete in the "scare the hell out of you" Olympics.

One of those high temperatured life frights happened when I was nineteen and wrapped in the spiritual strangeness of a late August New Mexico night.

That late summer sun is a killer when you are broke, out on the highway and livin' on your wits. Finally, that white orange ball piggy back slot drops behind the dark magenta horizon and the New Mexico desert evening air enters stage left with the first breeze since three days ago in Mexico.

Mexico, what a bust! My dreams of hookers, liquor, dope and food gave way to killer tequila hangovers, a lingering taste of bad food and social graces that quickly led a lessening wallet to, finally, no wallet at all. Get my drift, broke, without identification, dirty, hungry and hung over, my feet blistered from the sticky, taffy-hot highway.

Hitchhiking out of Mexico to Ohio required a few tricks not outlined in the manual of good scouting.

As I neared the outlying area of Tucumcarrie, that shallow turtle shell shaped glow of night lights met the quickly clouding desert sky. Tucumcarrie, maybe four miles off. What a place to rot. Not a single vehicle in the last twenty minutes, hoofing it into town in my salt ringed stained jeans, denim shirt and cheap and painful Acme boots with lots of miles.

The night sky became Biblically dramatic, forming long billowing tubes of darkening clouds heavy with rain. Clouds now seriously moving into the conductive glass furnace wall of desert air. The scent of fresh, drifting ozone widening the unsuspecting nostril, the exciting crack of summer storm desert thunder bolts like veined eagle claws road- mapping the sky. A bright, close by thundercap strobe lights the terrain, a flash glimpse of sleeping mountains and desert, pinpointed with Saguaro cactus and patches of silver sage.

Then it began, first like penny sized drops that steam dried on the still sticky asphalt, pumping the desert dust layer with small, donut shaped puffs of rain. Harder rain, until a full flash storm was dumping on Mr. Lucky without any cover. My clothes were now laminated to my perspiring body, sweat and rain burning my eyes and now soaked boots threatening a blister convention.

I sloshed into Tucumcari, seeking any shelter from the storm. Just over the edge of the City limits, I saw a police cruiser slow across the boulevard and one of those southwest, donut subscribing lawmen was looking me over. Smelling the vagrancy charge and the county work farm, I quickly cut back a block to an alley.

There near the end of the street next to that stretch of open desert, it looked like some sort of two level house or hotel. Run down, not maintained but sure looked dry inside. Frozen in the droplets, I quickly decided to at least try for a dry lobby or a roof overhang.

Through the smoke smeared window the lobby was deserted. A card table with several dominoes, four, torn well stained oversized chairs and a sloppily hand lettered "ring buzzer for room key after 10:00 p.m." sign. I took the creeping wood stairs to the second level corridor, if lucky, my home for the night.

A single center corridor, full length with a partially lit exit sign and grime stained room doors each with the splintered scars of tire iron and pry bar history. Chips of molded yellow paint loop curled from the ceiling and the three flickering flourescent light ballasts buzzed like barber shears. A well peed upon and worn carpet runner paved this upper level transient highway, further decorated with cigarette burns and dark who knows stains.

Exhausted, wet and dirty, I wrapped myself in the single window drape and laid mid- corridor against the wall. Under the charm of the urine odor and buzzing lights, I fell into restless sleep.

"Margaret, Margaret," he moaned from his sour breathe, a dribble of spittle bubbling over his purpled lower lip. Fully on the floor, next to me, hugging me, face to face, the derelict with the fallen eyes and the skin lesions on his forehead, cheeks and hands, was intent on sealing me into his mental health cocoon. As he lightly shook with each word, his head rolled shoulder to shoulder, exposing clumps of missing hair left with patches of veined albino like tissue.

The hair stood. I two footed the corridor in my streaming drapery cape and straight lined three blocks at full speed, stopped and gasped, "Who the hell was that?"

DRUGSTORE COWBOY

There exists a very brief flash of teenage time among American boy-men, the crazed rights of passage rituals era that exists during the learner's permit, Wonder Bread days of youth. The drugstore cowboy know-it-all, too proud to ask days of early manhood.

As the four of us shuffled, spat and strained to become adult males, to shed the tell tale snakeskin of innocent boyhood, we took our early evening positions below the buzzing blue and white fluorescent curved neon letters of Schumann Drugs.

Leaning against the black, specular polished granite of the local drugstore facade, we were poised to view every store patron and share our comments. Part of our youth guidance systems: visual review, voiced opinion, consensus or disagreement, all in the lingo of our practiced street slick jargon, seasoned well with hand gestures, compound cuss words, Lucky Strikes smoke and target spitting.

The revolving aluminum clad entry door beckoned our continuous review of the extensive magazine rack. Sweet, fresh smelling glossy printer's ink of Motor Trends fastest muscle cars, Field and Streams latest rifle and scopes with Wham-o slingshots on the last page and, most importantly, the skin magazine section, where the real stuff really was. Where all adolescent male conjecture, no matter how peculiar, was given the reality camera test.

Who were these girls and can they really get that big breasted by drinking lots of milk? And some of them look pretty mean, maybe just cause they're naked.

The white smocked pharmacist with the five o'clock shadow always dishes up the evil eye if we browse too long, but we can cover a lot of visual terrain in ten minutes. The shape of curved butts, nipples and custom cars usually carried the day.

Artie, one of our group's self appointed eleven year old sex authorities, convinced some that the larger the woman's breasts, the better the sex; further, women occasionally had babies through their breasts.

Ribbing me quickly with his elbow, Artie nodded towards the store entry, "There," he whispered, as an overweight woman in her mid seventies shuffled from the door in her flattened bunny slippers, tented in a print pattern with large breasts understandably swaying near the fifty yard line. Artie muffled his squeal, "God, look at those, why she's probably the best sex in town," to which we all kind of muttered, "Uh huh."

Before he had a license Mike managed to get his mother's car by pushing it down the driveway and starting it a block away, then drove it four blocks to the drugstore parking lot. There we sat, four of us in the new Pontiac Bonneville hardtop, windows down, duck tails combed, cigarettes in our tee-shirt arms, aftershave and ready for action but still no license.

Artie's older brother would buy us our cigarettes but tonight we chipped in for four cigars, a mix of clear cellophane wrapped thin and stubby stogies.

First one out of the car buys medium sized custard cones at the Dairy Queen. As windows were gasket closing we Ohio blue tip matched our ready cigars and grey blue bearded curls of first fragrant, then stinging, cigar smoke filled the car interior. The thicker puffs gave way to a solid tobacco cloud layer, thick enough to block vision in our watering eyes and start Tom's cough. Once the coughing started, we all knew the custard was near. Trial by cigar smoke, not a pleasant idea.

The drugstore days ended with our first driver's licenses and cars: the first instant magic of mobility, the drugstore anchor cut, free to take our stuff to the streets with an all new game of people and places.

The highlight of the drugstore chapters ended with the secret, dumb and scary 503 Club. Only four of us were members and hindsight tells me a Higher Being was silently caretaking me during these challenging times.

The 503, as in fifty miles per hour and three in the front seat. The requisite to do this included Tom Okey and his '51 Ford Tudor, a six pack of beer lifted from someone's back porch, lots of cigarettes and a good mix of blind courage and stupidity.

After chugging the lukewarm beers and pulling onto the deserted airport asphalt roadway with three in the front seat and the newie by the rider's door. Held steady at fifty, it begins, without losing speed, the rider takes the driver's position and everyone rotates sharing the steering wheel and gas pedal. The rider exits the window, slides over the hood and windshield, reenters the car through the driver's window. The key is to stay low, use exterior mirrors, wiper blades and hood vents carefully, move slowly and oh yeah, really concentrate.

Methodically back pedaling over the patchwork of my life, I squint and still see four faces glowing under the blue hued drugstore signage, a shared card in our lifetimes, a farewell salute to youth, a brief huddle before we silently split and began our more serious adult life games.

CAVALRY BUTTONS

Both in their early twenties, the two lanky Mississippi-born brothers squinted in the relentless, scorching, southern Arizona sun. Desolate, pancake flat terrain with occasional horse high, sandstone mesas, each geological time-locked layers of sienna, magenta and unexpected blue-green sparkling mica.

Nudging the eastern edge of the deceitfully dangerous Sonora Desert, only eighty miles north of Mexico, the language of cool and shade is unspoken here and water is king.

Nothing has the courage to exist here except scorpions, dwarfed mesquite, Gila monsters and uninvited sidewinders. Gorgeous in a graveyard sort of way, yet proven unforgiving and deadly on horseback for the unprepared and inexperienced.

Without great care, the blistering heat and yellow-white sun can simmer and sizzle a man's logic and draw him to the sandy mirage of unwitnessed, parched, desert death.

Distance here is measured by sunrises, sunsets and water required by man and his horse.

Cyrus and Virgil, a long way from the acquired comforts of southern-lush, Mississippi back country, yet pocketing eighty dollars per month in gold coin as forward scouts for the U.S. Cavalry. Nothing like this back in Mississippi, yet scouting for the

Army was like an extended bayou hunting and trapping journey without the whiskey.

Good at their jobs, and two days ahead of their mounted regiment, they carefully studied a passable horse trail, one rimming the desert, free of hostile Indian ambush sites, and with rare water runoff likely trapped in the deeper mesas.

The compass points were simple: ride to the water, usually locked below the higher, more muscular stone outcroppings. A two hour ride to the jagged dome left of that large mesa, almost certain to be water there.

Their chestnut horses glistened with a light sheen of sweat as they almost mechanically plodded a straight line toward the heat distorted mesa. The "U.S.A." steel stamped into the saddle matched the deep brand on the horse's flanks; flanks crossed with leather tack, saddlebags bulging with full Army issue, a burden for animal and man in this staggering blast furnace.

Their dark blue uniforms were caked with a light crust of blown dust and dried sweat; light yellow shoulder epitaphs and double breasted brass buttons glistened in the sun like the occasional glint from the rifle scabbard cradling the lever action 30-06 carbine rifle. Grimy sweat burned their eyes as they light-headily dreamt toward the stone cooled water.

The dark, copper-skinned Indian braves were finely tuned to the harsh, biting desert terrain. The Spirit of the Desert was their God, the sacred desert beauty and secrets were their life, and the Western Apache stubbornly protected his private, moonscaped wonderland.

Night Wolf and Red Sun, young Apache warrior braves, muscular, agile, both successful hunters, taught by the elders to trap, kill, hide, and use the magic of the desert's special plants to heal and find the truth. This was Apache country, born to the earth bloodline, connected to the many desert mysteries, not a place for warring Pima braves, not a place for murdering Quechan warriors on ponies, and definitely not a place for the white man with his deadly firestick.

Feasting on shredded rabbit and corn mash, the village ringed the flame lapping firepit as the chanting and dancing began. Nearly a full moon, with words of courage and tribal pride from the elders, chants from the squaws, and blessing of the weapons and passing of the pipe among the warrior braves.

The warrior dance reflected dark, firelit eyes and high cheekbones, boldly pigmented with ground roots and clays of yellow, red, and black in lightning bolt patterns: the signs of war. War ponies were given final deep drafts of water from gourds carried by the children and moonlit pony flanks were given a white clay handprint and red lighting bolt.

The two braves danced to the drumming, chewed the desert root and shared the pipe; warring euphoria and albino moonlight cascaded over them as they mounted their ponies, chests expanded with Apache pride.

Night Wolf and Red Sun spoke tracking and warring with Learned instincts, not words. As boys and young braves, they learned everything together: use of the bow, tomahawk, knife and pikestick, trapping their first wolf, the pain of snake bites, finding the secret water caves, droughts, tribal massacres, disease and living the Apache calloused life of just enough, while wasting nothing.

The early, purple sun rose with both braves miles from the tribe, covering the last of their water gourds with flat shards of dusty sandstone, a hidden supply of water for their return trip.

Traveling light, their unshod ponies were guided over rock washes and wind washed stone slabs to limit rising trail dust and minimize their horizon profiles.

Muscular Apache thighs gripped saddleless war ponies with a single rawhide lead banding the ponies' jaws just behind the nostrils. Simple hide sandals, a doeskin loincloth with braided leather tie, a small pouch of mesquite beans, a warrior head ornament of white flicker feathers with black tips, a lashed water gourd and small leather spirit bag traveled with each brave, as well as their weapons of choice.

Night Wolf prized his bear jawbone handled knife, the razor sharp blade now sleeping in the decorative quilled sheath had a developed taste for human and animal blood. His feathered war lance, light and balanced, was deadly. The shaft smooth for throwing, the blade edge jagged for tearing.

Red Sun knew the spirit of his pipe tomahawk; he and the weapon whispered death thoughts as he honed the shining blade edge. The smoothness of the handle was decorated with brass tack and Cavalry buttons with a lightning bolt deeply etched into the blood stained blade face.

No bows this warring party, not a match for the white man's rifle; close, surprise combat would be the order of deadly red and white business.

Red Sun instinctively dismounted and crouched as he pointed to the barely visible thin strand of rising dust against the cloudless, liquid blue sky. Two mounted bluecoats, very distant, riding directly toward the large water cave. Apache instincts immediately surfaced, the brave's nostrils widened as the invitation for desert murder quickly arrived.

Much closer to the precious water cave, the Indians carefully led their patched, colored war ponies to the far side of the massive mesa, rawhide tethering their ponies' rear legs and nostrils, where movement, smell or sound could prove deadly.

Tracklessly, the braves cat-stepped to the sandstone bowels of the cave. Eyebrowed by a jutting stone shelf-water-pool of spring fed saving liquid edged with shadowed tufts of olive-yellow algae and a stand of tube reeds. A level platform of stone met the water line, offering perfect access for man and horse. The reeds and algae were extra thick by the platform edge: and after spotting the Cavalry scouts at one quarter mile, Apache cunning accelerated.

Leaving no tell-tale moist footprints on stone, the braves crouched-skirted to the rear of the pond. Not raising the muddy bottom, pond edge mud was smeared on both faces, necks and lower arms. Then, with pike spear and tomahawk, Night Wolf and Red Sun slow-motioned themselves among the reeds. With weapons poised like fallen statues, they oozed just below the waterline. With squinted mud-stained eyes barely above the water, the braves controlled their breathing through the hollow reed tubes, cocked and deadly still, straining for the sound of horseshoe on rock, a voice, an order or shadow.

Two sharp shoe clips on the stone, then a winnowing Cavalry horse smelled the water. Both riders side cantered to the water's edge, freeing the reins; the tired horse heads lowered to drink.

The braves seized the perfect moment of opportunity. Freed by the now churning pool and bending reeds, the warriors sprung forward with high, chilling war whoops.

The art of killing, grasping the nostril and bit of a terrified horse while murdering its rider in one lethally graceful motion.

Night Wolf plunged the feathered pike spear deeply through Virgil's stomach, burying the spearhead beyond the string-leather bandings. Virgil's eyes rolled, coughing blood with his final breath, he splashed face down in the mud-reddening pool.

Red Sun, with reins and weapon in hand, seated the sun glinted arch of his tomahawk just above Cyrus's left temple, jettisoning a long thin spurt of blood over the rocks and horses. Before the droplets could land, Red Sun's knife buried in Cyrus's back, just above the beltline.

Wet, mud crusted and splattered with blood and skull fragments, the adrenaline pumped braves yelped while quickly tethering the excited Cavalry horses.

Dragging Virgil from the pond, they placed both scouts face up, then dropped on their chests, cleaving and rip slashing their scalps, knotting the blood soaked hair to their loincloth bands.

Red Sun fetched their hidden ponies as Night Wolf cut off all uniform brass buttons, all belt buckles, spurs, bridle bits and saddle sheet leather. He then pulled the still seething bodies to the sand and rinsed the blood from the rocks.

Cyrus and Virgil were tied behind the two new pack horses and dragged to cover any tracks to the next dried deep wash. There, Red Sun and Night Wolf shallow buried uniforms and saddle bags, leaving Cyrus and Virgil, nude, face up and very dead.

Just before riding to the first water gourd with two strong horses, matched repeating rifles and a bag of brass buttons, Night Wolf and Red Sun paused and praised their enemies' warrior spirit and from their spirit bags drew a small pinch of tobacco, smudging the upper lip of Mississippi's Best while placing a small, polished flat stone on each forehead.

ANT LIFE

We are the proud living symbol of a nation of unity, individually minute, but collectively able to provide gigantic results, biologically cataloged as Formicidae by you humans, and commonly refered to as ants.

My name is Red and I am the unit commander of a 130 ant crumb train labor force, part of a regional ant colony of approximately 18,000 with a fairly complex social organization. We are intricately networked by an infinite number of world wide colonies from Africa to Anchorage with the single mission of survival, eat or be eaten.

Secretly headquartered beneath the cracked concrete floor slab of the Hershey Chocolate Company in Pennsylvania with strategically placed outposts below the Pentagon, White House and New York Stock Exchange, we are politically and socially world wise.

Each individual colony is similarly structured with three groupings: sniffer ants, crumbline laborers and support services.

Scouting sniffer ants, sometimes too aggressive and socially brash, are responsible for ferreting out our never ending quest for crumbs and sugar. Posing upright on two rear legs, sniffers stand motionless and test the air for sugar odors, a barely audible clicking sound and light salivating of the front mandible usually indicate the location of a newly found crumb or sugar vein. As sniffers, they command a special social respect.

Shift work crumb line laborers are our greatest force, moving mountainous veins of crumbs and sugar crystals to our heavily guarded food bank. Crumb laborers are also our social blue collar class, with a do or die, work hard-play hard credo. As an incentive, crumb liners are bonused daily with three brown sugar crystals if the shift has moved at least 8500 granules. Such bonus granules are usually consumed at shift's end at the Red Ant Lounge: a dark, crystalized nest, complete with full sugar crystal service, piano bar, toilet compartments and exaggerated brown crystal story telling.

Since illegal dealing of brown sugar crystals is sometimes rampant at the lounge, bonused ants are searched at the door and if found high on brown sugar are admitted to our support services rehabilitation center for crystal abuse.

Our most cherished holiday, the annual viewing of the Queen, is attended by all. We dutifully bow as she passes with her protective oversized lancer guards. The dream of every crumb liner, with her perfect gauze glycerine transparent wings, slender body and carefully corn rowed leg hair, she is the centerfold of the entire salivating colony. She was born to please. After her passing, a flurry of snifer ants hopelessly comb the ground for any fallen hair follicles.

Politically we can impact the world in seconds but prefer to merely monitor man's many peculiarities. By gnawing and reconnecting a red telecommunication line beneath the White House, we once spliced the President mid call to the building janitor and later transferred all morning New York Stock Exchange transactions to the Boy Scouts of America.

A genuine work ethic exists since all non performing ants or those too feeble to work are dismembered and eaten.

We dream of gooey chocolate cake on paper picnic plates, relish the thought of leftover barbeque sauce and fear commercial ant killer, inquisitive children with magnifying glasses and stamping feet and, of course, the ever dreaded ant eater.

Well, there is the signal; gotta go now, the new shift is about to begin. By the way, as we see it, a nuclear holocaust would kill all ants as well as mankind, wouldn't it?

CLASS REUNION

The ritual of the aging sniffing dog contest, a chance to compare the social status quo, families, divorces, deaths, dreams, successes, failures, all featured at the highly anticipated class reunion.

Who is fatter, balder, much older looking or walking differently. The couples nursing their drinks while checking their watches; the couples near the edge of the dance floor, haven't danced all night and have that I'm old before my time far off stare. They have moved to the next tier, resolved to move toward death in a passive fashion without any pomp or circumstance.

Others chicken clutch for youth as the battle between young and old rages, a battle sometimes well camouflaged but never fully hidden. Look at her: she has had her eyes, chin and breasts enhanced, see, at the neckline, and his hair piece doesn't blend at the side burns. What an unlikely assortment of homosapiens yet a great slice of mid western Americana.

Tom Bell, now a very successful investment banker, looking pretty constipated in that gray pin stripped suit and armed with that squeaky, little frumpy wife. Now the model of corporate soldiering, he is an about face reversal of his academic yesteryears. Once a tough, street fighter, dirty tricks bully with an attitude, now the milk toast king of conventional boredom.

Falling out of the late 50's like a vending machine stale candy bar, Tony DeOreo stood out among the gawking group like a drunken priest, outfitted in black leather cycle chaps, metal studded boots and a black sleeveless tank shirt with Andy's Speed Shop in screaming flaming yellow letters. His grease rimmed broken fingernails and slipping wrench knuckle scars attested to his motor head passion for speed and street racing machinery. "Say man," he began, "remember that '32 sedan you had," and his monologue began: prototype composite tubular racing frames, performance cams and cranks, gear ratios, trick fuels, on and on marching unto street coup nirvana. His greased Presley like forehead locks bobbed with each comment as I side stepped toward the bar, leaving the 61 year old juvenile delinquent hot rodder still at the starting line of life.

Still the sought after cheer leader wet dream beauty queen of the Lincoln Lions, Veronica Cole, of course, at the center of the mirror sparkling studded dance floor. There she is close up and personal: what radiantly tight skin, those curves, her smile, very white teeth and a very large diamond ring. As she spun to the later evening dated rock and roll rhythms, her slit to the hip black sequined cocktail dress became a waste high Bermuda fan, revealing very shapely legs in black patent leather spikes. As her dress helicoptered, the men on the dance floor rolled their guppy like eyes her way. Well, like they say, "Once a queen, always a queen."

As the evening unfolded, I completed my obligatory honey bee flower to flower introductions and small talk chit chat with those I once shared math, history and science classes. Stepping back into the time capsule, carrying my precious sweet youth memories in my aging life bag, locking tonight safely away, forever captured in pure clear high school amber.

AFTERLIFE

Some say that when you die you are just plain dead meat, gone, no more, lights out, game over. Other late life sinners, and desperate, card-carrying, religious enrollees have placed heavy side bets that another life hereafter awaits them, although the very small print of the next life warranty does not guarantee the specifics of your return as either a reconstituted king or a common garden slug.

As you, I have toyed with the notion of a reincarnated status. Next lifetime around I'll order all the best stuff from the reincarnate catalog : happiness, intelligence, muscles, prosperity and good looks from that section where you select from the pattern book choices of skin color, hair type, teeth, eyes and other more private body features. Under no circumstances will I be returning with freckles or skinny legs.

Small cracks in this post mortem belief system began when I barely noticed what appeared to be a thin, flesh toned zipper on her back, just above the line of her swimsuit. With strengthening curiosity I later asked about the skin zipper. Seemingly embarrassed at first, she swore me to secrecy, then on a small sand spit she carefully demystified the entire life after process.

She was one of a small but very select group of reincarnates, one of those selected by the Man, to relive their life again on this planet as a different soul and in a somewhat different body.

Men and women selected for this special process were first life notorious for either their good or evil ways. You would certainly recognize some on the roster : Mother Teresa, Hitler, Joan d'Arc, Genghis Khan and Cleopatra, just to mention a few.

Shortly after the strange yet anticipated ring of the death alarm clock, the rebirthing begins with a new body selection at the next life storage plant, a windowless building refrigerated to 38 degrees Fahrenheit. Cataloged with great detail, each body skin suit, complete with hair and slightly blue hued fingernails, hung limp on a shoulder rack with hundreds of number variations all mounted on a slow moving drycleaners conveyor belt.

All new body options were painfully considered by the Man, a choice one merely accepted as the numbered disc in the perspiring wet palm revealed the matching skin suit number. The conveyor lurched to a stop and there it was, your never been worn, new life on a hanger.

Life slowly began to change within the skin suit as the spinal zipper was tightly closed and latched. The life starter's gun was fired and reincarnated living began, though certainly not the same.

I suppose the newly launched personalities were both appropriate and startling, as if the Man may have had some soul justice reward or payback attitude in mind.

Worthy of mention, some personalities now existed in stark contrast to their previous lives. Just think of it, Adolph Hitler, now a midnight shift, bed pan-toting female nurse in the elderly special care unit. Finally humbled and polite as she carefully emptied the endless brown liquid rainbows from the strangely curved stainless steel pans. The only remaining remnant of the earlier Adolph was her barely noticeable Charlie Chaplin mustache shadow.

Mother Teresa's reconstituted life now included chairing the board of directors as Chief Financial Officer of an international energy conglomerate, diverting millions in unrecorded assets to poverty organizations in India and Africa. Some earlier habits die hard as she tapped her now lacquered nails on the thirty-two seat board room bird's eye maple table. Finally alone, she quickly gathered the special pastries and untouched finger sandwiches from the very corporate cadenza into her large Italian leather briefcase for later distribution to the rough cut band of street people.

The once frail Michael Jackson, now a 280 pound hooked nose wrestler, famed for his red sequined shorts and white glove, became the bruising brute of Madison Square Gardens but was temporarily barred from the ring, accused of kissing Hulk Hogan after he successfully applied the sleeper hold.

In today's fast moving world, death has become both fashionable and politically correct, based on our bulging cemeteries and smoke oily crematorium chimney flues. The "D" word appears to be just plain unavoidable. We all wanna know what the future holds for us behind mortality door number three be it prince, pauper, spiritual leader or the dreaded garden slug.

Aging, I more stubbornly strain to bolt the door from the now lightly knocking death angel while hoping to be dealt just one more life card. Truth is, I'll take any available next life ticket rather than the infinite, black drone of decaying nothingness.

While I momentarily daydreamed death at the bar, an attractive, middle aged woman introduced herself and flattered me by asking to dance. Stepping onto the small polished floor, we cordially locked new fingers and my right hand dutifully found her upper back. She certainly reminds me of someone, such familiar features, yet I just can't place her. She gave me a very understanding wink as my fingertip pads lightly brushed the very top of her spinal skin zipper.

LIFE BOOK

Unlatching the dome topped lacquered trunk, the lid stretched its musty scented, brass hinged jaw and fresh air clashed with cherished family heirlooms. Photographs, awards, long forgotten memberships, Boy Scout badges and a cadre of rarely to be seen assorted articles documenting my past, like so many social highway mile markers.

Each item knee jerked me into a thin razor slice of my history, a staccato like visit with a vivid chip of my life. Ah, what joys and pains live within the gray folds of our brain's unerring memory bank. Those memory bankers, well, they're most incredible and never forget a thing.

At the bottom corner of the trunk, face down, a previously undiscovered leather bound book. I gasped at the gold leaf, embossed cover title, "Life Instructions for Bill McCluskey," a how to life manual, complete with diagrams and directions for a happy life. Note, contains prioritized information, not transferrable, to be presented at birth.

Damn! I've never even seen this, no wonder life has been this way. Hell, I've been livin all along like this without my instruction book.

Erratically thumbing through the chapter titles, it became clear this information was tailor made for me, a chronology of do's and don't's from birth to death. Special detailed steps were provided in order to be loving, healthy, successful and happy, additionally, how to avoid pain, heartaches and life's lessor murmurs of disappointment.

The love and intimacy chapter would have been especially handy. There it was, clear in typeset black and white with associated dates. Listed in the don'ts column: don't date Vicky Scott, she's a tramp, 1956; don't get into the back of the Ford coupe with Sandy, 1958; don't marry Susan, it will end in divorce, get an abortion; and Miriam, simply just stay totally away from her.

Do keep promises, remember birthdays, tell people you love them, don't drive drunk, enjoy your surprisingly short life journey, don't get too serious and, if you must go, then go to the Asshole Olympics by yourself.

Educational tips were abundant and there glaring right at me, I knew it: don't take calculus and organic chemistry during the same semester; don't try and cram for the Art History final; and, above all, don't cheat in Mr. Ashby's Algebra class, don't go to Architectural graduate school, get an MBA instead at Stanford. Finally, don't steal any clay or eat paste in kindergarten class.

Don't eat too much fast food, skip the coffees and stay away from double shots of Tequila Gold with frosty beer chasers before sunset. Do eat your spinach and brussel sprouts, grill fresh fish, savor exotic fruits and tell your body how much you love it. Rest and exercise well, dream long and stay well away from motorcycles, heroin, prostitutes and black tipped reef sharks.

Do patiently listen to all spiritual stories, dream often, chant, pray, drum, dance and sing to your spirit Gods. Don't curse or threaten God, after all, there is that outside possibility, why chance it.

Do love your parents, treat them like gold even though they may have read the wrong child rearing books. Get your arms around them, tell them what a great job they've done and help them peacefully launch their death boats. Lastly, don't bury your parent's car keys in the sand box or throw raw eggs at the monster in the ceiling.

The last chapter in my life series, "Death and Dying", was torn from the book, only stubbles of pages left to chart the how and why of my death dance. Someone must have these pages but until I find them, I'll just write the final chapter my way.

BEETLES

"That's the very last of it, 4 feet wide, 24 feet long, 1/4" heavy gauge mesh, oughta cover maybe six or seven windows," growled Irv as he flopped the galvanized roll onto the cashier's counter at Irv's Ranch Supply and Hardware. Two miles south of Route 22, a straight pencil rod slot through southern Wyoming. Southern Wyoming: gorgeous, still spirited Indian country of naturally sophisticated nothingness.

You can scream your lungs out everyday and no one will hear you in a lifetime.

"I'd a ordered a mess of screenings and fasteners if I'd a known earlier about all this screen slashing. Damn near sold most everything out first of the week since those problems late last Friday night at the Crowley and Chester ranches."

Went out at day break with Sheriff Skinner, damnest thing you ever saw, slashed and twisted all the lower screens off the house. Looked like some pointed horn or pincher gouged the lapped siding and left a sticky slime near the kitchen.

Late last Tuesday night, Irv gingerly edged the old Chevy Apache pickup into the once busy loading area of the abandoned gravel pit. With lights out, the tires creeping towards the deadly edge of the pit, some 80 feet below.

There, on the moonlit gravel bar maybe thirty or forty of them and eight or ten others scaling the opposite pit wall.

Like an acoustical amplifier, the pit walls ricocheted with deep humming harmonics and a rising and falling, crisp, clicking sound-orchestration for a thousand castanets.

Damn frightening looking. An upright, man sized beetle with enlarged head, compound eyes, active antennas and an obvious set of very nasty looking pinchers, the sharp kind with those jagged edges. The dark cordovan oversized head, a lightly oiled thin shell with a honey combing of raised veins, veins expanding and glowing and somehow synchronized with the clicking crescendos.

Dark, deer thin legs and front limbs gave the armored beetles great power and agility; however, the beetles were committed, passionate and driven by one thing only. They were blinded by their total addiction to cocoa and their lives were totally dedicated to nocturnal pursuits of the wonderful dark colored powder.

When I first spotted one in the headlights, it was just a large beetle; but now it's clear they are much larger and bigger than the dog.

It's just a matter of time until they are drawn by western fry kitchen odors to each ranchhouse.

The dog and I instantly hit the bedroom floor when the cable tension screen door left its hinges to the 3:00 a.m. drone of the cocoa beetles harmonic penetration. The front door gave way to rapid puncture tearing and the first salivating beetle pinned the dog under the collapsing kitchen table. The second and third beetle visitors charged, wedging me behind the refrigerator door.

The house quickly filled with the echoing beetle harmonics. Investigation and pincher crushing of most everything occurred immediately. Canned fruits and sauces hissed as surgical pinchers punctured metal like foil. Everything thoroughly sniffed by the rubber rope like beetle antennas before crushing.

Their swamp breath and lobster like pinchers loomed in my face as the nasal antenna scanned my face and neck. First sputtering a nest of bubbles, then turning, the beetle was fortunately not interested in the taste of fresh people.

After endless minutes accordion squashed behind the refrigerator door, I gazed through my now punctured kitchen wall to the living room.

What a transformation: all the living room furnishings had been pinched to a strangely arranged pyramid of broken chair legs, upholstery bits, glass fragments and carpet scraps. All piled over the television set, now dragged to the center with the flat portion of a black lacquered end table crowning the pyramid. On the top set a very heavily punctured can of Hershey's Cocoa, a ragged box of chocolate chip cookie mix and half a bag of mini marshmallows, an apparent sugar altar.

The beetles stationed the television channel to the children's cartoon network and attentively relinquished from clicking during the cartoons, but went absolutely wild during the forever interruptive commercial ads for sugared cereals, sugar injected snacks and, most of all, ads for layered candy bars.

After each televised candy ad the cocoa beetles would click with great joy, secretly wink at one another then faithfully, touch their antennae to the cocoa spoils atop their ritual pyramid. Signaling approval, several beetles ashamedly dripped drops of a sticky secretion on the gashed carpet after their cocoa hit.

The cocoa beetles disbanded as rudely as they appeared, leaving in unison shortly after the highlight commercial of the evening, the Oreo Cookie ad. When the cookie was halved the clicking crescendo began and all took ritual pyramid cocoa and left the floor with small puddles of cocoa beetle approval.

Heat just around the corner, the rising hot tip of the Wyoming summer sun gobbling the last of the defenseless magenta stained morning air.

Layered against that pancake flat horizon, there to the left, see 'em, like the steel lugs of a zipper, hundreds of disappearing pin heads marching single file into the liquid sun. Methodical and determined, the cocoa beetles trudged eastward, nasal antennas straining for the slightest suggested scent of cocoa and a change of direction.

CHAIRMAN OF THE BOARD

It was bound to happen sooner or later; the problem is we all bet on later and were wrong. Bio engineering and genetic technology have drunkenly sprinted to limitless, sometimes unpredictable, variations of humans, biological combos, if you will. Surgical laser attachments or SLP's are common now throughout metropolitan North America as well as portions of Europe and Japan, providing almost instant fusion surgery of selected animal components with humans. Now, Cisco Systems of the tech bulging Silicone Valley has developed and distributed the Genetic Engineering vending machines, quite an inventive and life changing piece of now public equipment.

I cautiously approached the newly installed machine at the Broadway and 8th subway station at 3:00 in the morning. Free of rude commuter hordes or distractions, only the sporadic whimpers of a newspaper wrapped derelict laying in a shallow puddle on the hose wet platform. There it set: flush, brushed stainless steel face with black rubber grommet set vandal proof glass, an internal step in hermetically sealed interview, test cubicle, phone booth size but fully, hygienically outfilled with bone scanners, organ profiling, muscular-skeletal analysis and a full animal-human compatibility work up. Moments after genetic profiling, verification of components and method of payment is completed, including waiving genetic engineering of any liability as a consequence of newly grafted animal parts.

Once signed: head, chest, leg and arm padded restraints firmly position you in the now horizontal tilting metal tube frame surgical chair. The polished small highly sophisticated operatory is sealed with a thin blue fog of monitored anesthesia while numerous computer guided scalpels and injection syringes unrhythmically appear then quickly retract from patterned wall openings of the near phobic operating capsule.

Rollover, monitoring screens above impulse spit neon red, blue and green progress reports as a final hygienic heat fusion concludes the process.

Kind of funny: I stood on the nearly dry concrete floor, damp footprints into the machine looked like a man's size eleven, but the tracks leading from the machine look like a large ostrich footprint or some sort of rapture bird. Guess that could account for that sharp female scream heard earlier at the dark end of the platform.

Satisfied with the alleged success of the genetic vending machine, I dreamt of personal changes for myself that were limitless - just imagine: crowding my way to the front of the beer concession lines at the opening Mets game with my bared gorilla chest; chasing and tackling a mid town purse snatcher with my cougar legs, or impressive love making with a little genetic help from the black stallion; and directly addressing aggressive drivers with my double rhino horn. Hell, all it took was a stack of money and the imagination to be all you can be.

As many of the stuffy, liver spotted live forever board members, I typically detested these long, argumentative shareholders meetings. All the stock manipulation power proxies and secret voting, capped with Cuban cigars, single malt scotch and razor sharp lies delivered from unblinking steel gray corporate eyes. These poisonous meetings simply had to change at any cost.

Glancing in the full length mirror of the empty polished marble corporate bathroom, I first grimaced then smiled and winked. The wiry stubble of hair on my new boars head outlined the extended jaw; the bead perspiring snout was flanked by two corkscrew like tusks and rows of crooked, albino stumped teeth, all highlighted with a heavy bellowing of barnyard breath and occasional sticky webs of generated saliva. Guess I could hide the pointed hairy tail up under the coat or in the trouser leg, but the boars head is gonna require more than make up.

God, this genetic engineering vending machine stuff is absolutely genius, really a Godsend if you are well heeled at $5000/component.

After years, finally the Board of Directors will certainly feel my wrath tonight, not the normally meek and quiet Mr. Vernon P. Nuttley, II, but the new me with my newly acquired gorilla arms, Black Forest Boars head and water buffalo hoofs. No one dare challenge my proxy vote or I'll savagely crush the oval birds eye maple directors table to splinters.

I can't wait, it will be my shocking surprise entry. I'll scare the shit out of Harold, board president, and Jerald that wimp of a chairman can just sniff my piggy breath.

There through the crack, is that Harold, looks like his suit and shoes but, Oh Christ! Harold has a tigers head and he's growling, and the lobster claw hands are intimidating enough but tough to control a pen. And, oh great, there's Jerald the wimp, but he sure walks differently in those kangaroo legs, yet the beaver head with those teeth, it's like him, the bean counting accountant.

What to do now. Only a half hour until the meeting - got it, that's it, superb one upsmanship, quick to the vending machine and an entire makeover. It's war now, I'm ordering the full blown skunk outfit.

HANDS

Palm, four fingers and an opposable thumb, the free ends of our living forelimbs, our incredible hands. Used for far more than grasping and holding, they magically perform ballet like responses to our slightest brain commands. Great organic tools capable of almost anything from reverently nesting in prayer to strangling the air from an enemy's throat. Some with matted tufts of long curled hair, some with stone hard lacquered manicures, some with scars and tatoos, some ivory smooth delicate, yet all of them faithfully serving us without question.

Young, cocky and liquored up, a bragging unshaven trail gun slinger wraps his hand around the brimming shot glass while eyeballing the town's all business gunfighter. This instant hate hung heavy at the bar and was destined for the street. That right hand now fingering the smoothly filed steel hammer of the death barking forty four caliber Colt Peacemaker, then the slice cut 11 notches in the edge of the worn smooth hickory grip. Now, Hands, serious business: don't draw until you see the glint in his eye.

Aged, wrinkled hands with knobby joints, almost faded scars and protruding blue veins peppered with sun spots. Hands reverently folded in prayer, join with a quiet chaffing sound heard only by one's God. Symmetrically bonded, the upright hands tenderly and humbly transmit our most private wishes to a greater power.

Capital Billiards, a second story mid-Chicago pool room noted for high stakes games and out of state visitors. Timmy Betevania, a hot headed Sicilian local nine ball talent fingered the crease in his tailored made trousers, just breaking over the heel of his black, pointed, spit shined Stetson shoes. Lingering like a shadow at the polished newly felted Brunswick regulation table, he leaned under the harsh edge of the pool table light, silently placing five neatly folded hundreds on the rail edge. A chunky out of towner carefully eyed him, shuffled to the table, then covered his bet with a rubber banded clip of twenties. The thick, aging Italian visitor won the break and mechanically downed the first eight balls with deadly precision, but miscued and left the money ball against the opposite rail. A tough reverse bank shot, demanding total concentration. The hands knew it was show time, towel dried palms, a chalked cue stick held delicately firm, time to bank the nine into the corner pocket. Later these hands would put $1,000. into his pregnant Italian wife's pepper jar or be palms up as he explained away his Friday paycheck.

The warm embrace is responsive and she presses her full cleavage against me like a printing press. Our love temperatures steadily rise and our sexual arousal lights begin to flicker. Tracing the silken lines of the restricting bra, the flat small metal hooks are at last artfully freed with adolescent skill and a new plateau of excitement arrives in the form of two bobbing ivory breasts. The hands tenderly cup and mold the two pleasure domes and tweak the two pink rose buds. The hands like it here and decide to remain and play awhile.

The smooth, forest green velvet lined poker table, one of hundreds at the bell clanging, cocktail fueled casino, was host to cash clutching hands, hands from Asia to Alaska, constantly shuffle boarding neat stacks of chips and freshly cut card decks. Third from the left in the sport coat and extended French cuffs, he cooly palms an ace and a jack of diamonds from the previous deal. His pinky finger skillfully taps out the ace from under the French cuff as other unanticipated hands quickly join the game. These hands now on his elbows and the brief metallic flash of pit boss security handcuffs, bringing a swift sense of astonishment and helplessness to both hands.

When you think about them, hands are really the most incredible damn things, with some manicuring, an occasional band aid and hand cream, they articulate all tasks thanklessly and are definitely happiest when most tenderly clasped with others.

Printed in the United States
By Bookmasters